Nyenea

To Angela Kalmus

Nyenea

THE CHILD SOLDIER

• • •

Yurfee Binda Shaikalee

ISBN-13: 9780692463659
ISBN-10: 0692463658
Library of Congress Control Number: 2015920409
yurfee, Philadelphia, PA

This book is dedicated to memory of my late father, Mr. David Senvargbeh Shaikalee who was killed by NPFL rebels in Gbarnga, Bong County on July 12, 1994.

CHAPTER 1

• • •

MR. NUTEH MLEH HAILED FROM Gibi in Margibi County. He was the only child of his father, an old man called Nyenea Mleh, who was a farmer from the Gibi Mountain. Mount Gibi, as it is called, is one of the largest mountains in Liberia. The county was named after the mountain. The farmers there grew sugarcane, cassava, and rice. The largest employer in Mount Gibi was the German Rubber Plantation Company. There were mixed tribes in Mount Gibi, including Kpelleh and Bassa. Mr. Mleh and his wife were Kpelleh by tribe.

Mr. Mleh worked with the Bong Mining Company as an engineer. He and his family lived in Bong Town Horse Club, where only the senior staff of the company resided. Bong Town was one of the most beautiful housing estates in Liberia. Folks living in Bong Town were highly esteemed in Bong Mines. He had a lovely wife called Polan. They had four children: three beautiful girls (Neneh, Seanee, Jokata) and a boy who was their last child. The family lived a simple life but was among the affluent in Bong Mines.

It took a long time for them to have their son after their daughters. Mr. Mleh had wanted a boy child to carry on the family legacy. Polan asked her husband one night whether they should adopt a boy.

"No, we'll wait until God gives us a son," Mr. Mleh had said. They were members of the Baptist church of Nyenh. Because of their strong belief in God—that children came only from him—they had decided to wait.

On January 1, 1975, Polan gave birth to a boy. The event brought a lot of joy to the whole family. The oldest girl, Neneh, was nineteen years old and Seanee was eighteen. Both had completed their high school in Bong Town High School. The youngest daughter, Jokata, was sixteen years of age and a senior student at the same school. They all wanted a brother and had prayed for God to give them one. Every time the girls sat together, they always discussed having a brother, so the birth of their brother was really a day of celebration. They had a party in their house and brought lots of friends and relatives together. Their house was packed when the name of the child was announced.

"Our son's name is Nyenea. This means 'the world.' He is named after my father, who had wished for this day but died five years ago," Mr. Mleh said. The child looked just like his late father, old man Nyenea.

In 1980, Mr. Mleh bought five hundred acres of land in his village in Mount Gibi and started a rice and sugarcane farm. He built a six-bedroom house on the farm. In 1989, he started planning to resign from the Bong Mining Company and move with his family to the farm. He had told his wife about his plans but his wife was concerned about their oldest daughters, who were attending Cottington University College in Gbarnga, Bong County. Neneh was in her second semester, and Seanee was in her first semester. "My dear," said Polan to her husband, "I think we should send our daughters to my brother in the United States for their university education. Jokata will be finishing high school this year December."

"All right, my dear, but let's talk with your brother first and get his response."

Polan called her brother, Kiamu, in the United States, and he agreed that his nieces should stay with him.

Polan's parents were Mr. and Mrs. Fhan Sumo. They lived in Salala, Lower Bong County, after Mr. Sumo retired from the Firestone Rubber Plantation Company. Mr. Sumo and his wife, Leneh, were proud of their children's achievements. Polan and her brother, Kiamu, were the only children of their parents. Polan was the younger. In 1975, Kiamu traveled to the United States after high school to study on a scholarship from the Liberian government. Kiamu could not return in 1980 after the brutal coup d'e´tat that brought Master Sergeant Samuel Kayon Doe and the People's Redemption Council (PRC) to power. Because of the killings of many members of the former ruling government officials of True Wing Party (TWP) cabinet ministers, most Liberians living in exile decided not to return home in 1980.

Their daughters, Seanee, Jokata, and Neneh left for the United States on July 15, 1989. They were very sad to leave their little brother, who was fourteen years old. They had cried, hugged, and kissed at the Roberts International Airport before boarding PanAm.

● ● ●

Little Nyenea cried for his sisters all night until he fell asleep. Mr. Mleh and his wife were sad and happy that their girls were gone.

"It's the best we can do because schools are getting horrible in the country," Polan said.

"Yes, my dear. I'm glad to have you as my wife after twenty-one years of marriage, and if I was young again, I would still choose you out of millions," Mr. Mleh said to his wife.

"I love you too, dear," Polan said.

They had met when they were teenagers and fallen in love at the Samuel Grimes High School in Kakata, Margibi County. After completing high school, Mr. Mleh went to the Bong Mines Vocational Training Center, where he got an associate degree in mechanical engineering while Polan received an associate degree as a teacher after completing her studies at Kakata Rural Teacher Training Institute (KRTTI) in Kakata. They got married in 1968 upon the completion of their studies.

Both of their parents valued education and wanted the best for their children. Polan knew that her husband loved her. She earlier had a rival in high school called Loretta. Loretta was the most beautiful and brilliant girl on campus. She had all the boys falling head over heels for her. Loretta and Mr. Mleh had courted for some time in high school. They were the most popular students in school. Mr. Mleh was the best striker on the school football (soccer) team, and that made him very popular. Loretta was from an upper-class family that never allowed their daughter to hang around a native or bushman's son.

This was a common attitude of the so-called Americo-Liberian class before the overthrow of their hegemonic rule in 1980. A native was low class, poor, and a villager. Loretta's parents were Americo-Liberian descendants of free slaves from the United States who were resettled on the shores of Montserado River in Liberia in 1822 from the United States. They ruled the indigens of the land just as their colonial white masters had done in the United States. Loretta had gone for studies in the United States right after high school—something that was normal for their children.

Mr. Mleh was left with no alternative than to ask for Polan's hand in marriage. But that was behind them now as they had loved and cherished each other for the past twenty-one years. Polan knew only one man in her life: her husband.

● ● ●

Nyenea had the family to himself, and so he didn't feel alone.

"Our little Nyenea will have our attention now that he is alone. What should we do about his schooling out there on the farm now that he's in the ninth grade?" Polan asked her husband.

"He will attend Konola Mission next year, but in the meantime, you can conduct home studies," Mr. Mleh said.

Mr. Mleh resigned from the mining company in late July 1989. It was a hot day in October 1989 when the Mleh family moved to the farm. Nyenea was fascinated by the farm. The rice and cassava were ready for harvest. The sugarcane grew to full height. New rice, as the ripe rice is called in Liberia, is the best kind to eat or make into bread (rice bread), and harvest time is the best time to be on the farm. All of this had Nyenea so excited. He ate the roasted and boiled corn with eagerness. His father watched with delight as Nyenea enjoyed himself.

He had thought the farm would be too boring, but as it turned out, his son loved staying there. Nyenea had left all of his friends, playground, swimming pool, and sports behind. Instead, he had many questions for his father about rice, cassava, and sugarcane. The farm was remote compared to where they had lived in Bong Town for many years, but the family adjusted to it very quickly.

Mr. Mleh bought grinding machines for his rice and sugarcane. He was the only farmer with grinding machines in the entire Gibi clan. His investment in the machines paid off as soon as they were set up. Other farmers came to grind rice and sugarcane. The mill was expanded to accommodate more customers.

Mr. Mleh hired ten permanent workers to work on his farm and at the mill. He also hired day laborers to harvest the rice and cassava. He got so busy that he could not believe that there was so much to do.

His wife cautioned him about working too hard.

"Yes, I'll take it easy—but after I finish setting up the milling factory," Mr. Mleh said.

For two hours a day from Monday to Friday, Polan taught Nyenea at home. She had been a primary school teacher, but Nyenea thought she was too technical about everything. He'd always tried to play the mother-and-child game, which his mother never allowed in class. Nyenea was an A student, so his mother didn't have to shout much. They got along in class quite well.

Mr. Mleh came home one afternoon from Kakata, the provincial capital city, and announced the arrival of some letters with pictures from their daughters.

"Thank God for our girls. May the Almighty watch over them," Polan said. Nyenea too was happy to read a letter from his sisters.

Dear little brother,

We miss you so much. At times, we cry when we look at your picture. We're also praying for you to grow up as a disciplined young man. Please continue to be a loving and sweet little son to Mama and Papa. We love you, and God willing, we'll meet soon. The weather is very, very cold here. All the lakes and rivers in Minnesota state have turned to ice. We're getting used to it, but we hope to come back home to our hot sunny weather. We sent you a very special gift. Please take good care of yourself.

With love,
Neneh, Seanee and Jokata

The girls' gifts to Nyenea were a Nintendo game and a picture in a gold-plated frame. "I'll keep this picture for the rest of my life," Nyenea said to himself. The two older girls had gotten admission to university, and Jokata had completed high school, and they were all preparing for their first Christmas in the United States.

Mr. Mleh also started poultry and piggery farming. Mr. Mleh drew out a plan for the farm. "We have to support our girls in the United States and little Nyenea here with us. I want us to expand the poultry and make it bigger than the Brights' farm in Kakata. We have to buy one Hillux pickup truck to add to our old Nissan pickup truck. January 1990 will mark a new beginning on our farm." Mr. Mleh thought of having a good sale of chickens the following year. Their poultry would start producing eggs in six months, and he wanted to supply chickens to various supermarkets in Monrovia or the Bong Town supermarket.

Polan was glad to hear about what her husband had planned.

The workers liked Nyenea and answered his questions about the hens, roosters, and pigs. Dekie Woodor was one of the boys working on the farm, and he took to Nyenea on their arrival. Every time Nyenea came over to visit, they would spend lots of time together. Polan encouraged him to come over to the house for lunch so that he and Nyenea could spend more time together. Nyenea had no playmates except for his parents.

Dekie's father had worked for the German Rubber Plantation Company as a rubber tapper until his death in a car crash in 1988. His mother had gone back home to Sanniquelle, Nimba County, with his two sisters, Zowahbah and Lulu. Nimba is home to the Gio and Mano tribes and borders Bong County. Dekie and his family were from the Mano tribe.

Dekie stayed behind to work and raise funds for his school fees in the Booker Washington Institute (BWI) in Kakata. He dropped out of school to work for a year before going back to complete the senior class.

"Where are your parents?" Polan asked Dekie one day.

"My father died last year, and my mother moved back to Sanniquelle with my sisters."

"Oh, I am so sorry about your father's death," Polan said. "How old are you?"

"I am nineteen, Ma."

"I want you to be a good example to our son because he's all we've got," Polan said.

Dekie was given a place to sleep on the farm, and he monitored three security guards at night. Dekie was loved by the family, and he went the extra mile to perform his best. Dekie saw to it that everything on the farm was OK every morning. He checked the poultry and the piggery, and he inspected the mill before work began. Nyenea asked his parents more than once for Dekie to move into the main house, but his parents asked him to wait until they got to know him better.

"My husband and I are very proud of you, and we are willing to support you in school if that's fine with you," Polan told Dekie one evening.

"I am very glad to hear such wonderful news, Ma. I would like to go to school," Dekie said.

Mr. Mleh asked some of the workers about Dekie, and they all spoke well of him. "He's hardworking and very serious about completing high school," a coworker, James said.

"I don't know why I started farming so late when I told you that I wanted us to marry and move to my parents' village to farm. I have always wanted to be on the farm. I want Nyenea to take over the farm after completing his university degree in agricultural science," Mr. Mleh said.

"Please allow our son to choose who he wants to be in the future. That was what my parents did to me when they said that I should be a teacher when I wanted to be a medical doctor. I still regret their decision for me, but I had to accept it because they were paying my school fees," Polan said.

"Oh, dear Polan. The boy is involved in everything out here as if he was born here," Mr. Mleh said.

"I remember growing up here in the village when I had to get up at four o'clock in the morning and travel three for four miles on foot to the farm with a basket of chickens on my head. We, the children, had to clear the dew that settled on the grass along the road. Those days were hard, and farming was so remote compared to what we have here. My father had other relatives' children living with us, and we also had to leave the farm by noon to go to school and return to the farm after school before coming back to town. It's not like that now, sweetheart. We're in a new age, and there's more money in farming than before. Besides, my father was always short of funds for our school fees. We're supporting our daughters in the United States and have a beautiful house to live in with piped-in water and electricity. I'm planning on buying us a satellite dish this Christmas season. In Bong Mines we watched CNN and BBC, and Sky Channel and Super Channel from the UK I am not keeping up with news much because of this job, but I will as soon as we get our dish," he explained to his wife.

Mr. Mleh liked to tell a story about when he was a kid on his family's farm. The story was about his laziness in felling a forest tree. He had gotten tired that day, and he asked his father for permission to go to the toilet. After two hours, there was no sign of him. Mleh was fast asleep on the other side of the forest, avoiding work. One of the hired workers felled a big tree that landed close by. A branch fell over him and had nearly frightened him to death! He had been so afraid that he cried out for help. When he was discovered later and pulled out, he'd lied and said that he had been to the toilet.

Mr. Mleh finished harvesting the rice and stored two thousand bags of seed rice and five thousand bags of clean grind rice.

"We'll sell some rice and plant three times as much as we had this year," Mr. Mleh informed his wife that night as they lay in bed. Nyenea was having problems with his skin after walking through the sugarcane farm.

"He's feeling feverish and needs to see a doctor," Polan told her husband.

"OK, you can take him to the Rennie Hospital in Kakata tomorrow and stop over at the supermarket to buy our weekly supplies," Mr. Mleh said to his wife.

The next day, they traveled to Rennie hospital in Kakata and came back with some medication for Nyenea.

"How are you, son?"

"I am fine, Papa, but my skin still itches."

"Next time you go to the sugarcane farm, you should wear long-sleeved shirts and long pants. I'll tell Dekie about that."

"Yes, Papa."

Mr. Mleh was very close to his son. He could not afford to see anything happen to him. They showered him with love. Nyenea reminded him so much of his late father. He would take the boy out to explain the crops to him and how they grew. He decided to put farming into his son, just as his father had done for him. His father had wanted him to study agricultural science after high school, but he had chosen engineering instead. He still had his regrets, but his wife had said that it was the will of God.

The Christmas week was very hectic. There were sales going on, and Polan prepared the house for guests and cooked Christmas food. The family went shopping in Monrovia on the December, 23, 1989. Mr. Mleh sent his daughters some money for Christmas and bought the satellite dish. There were lots of gifts for Nyenea, including a new BMX bike. Everything was prepared by Christmas Eve.

The family received a few family members and friends. Polan's mom was among the guests. Everyone was amazed to see the size of the farm. Along with Nyenea, Polan took her mother around that evening.

Ma Leneh was very fond of Nyenea. "Are you planning on sending Nyenea to a boarding school next year?"

"No," replied Polan. "We've decided to send him to the Konola mission nearby next year. He'll be starting the tenth grade."

"Nyenea, how old are you?" Ma Leneh asked.

"I am fourteen years old."

"Wow," exclaimed Ma Leneh. "You're a big boy! You were just few months old some years ago, and now you're a big boy! Look, Polan. You and your husband should do everything possible to discipline your son. Most young men are disrespectful today because of their upbringing."

"Yes, Mom. We're doing everything possible. Please remember us in your prayers every day."

"Your father and I have never ceased praying for all of you."

"Thanks, Mom." Polan felt like a child before her mom again.

She turned her face away quickly to hide her tears. "Mom, why did you come without Papa?"

"Your father said that he's not happy about Christmas this year. He's a bit troubled. I tried to persuade him, but he said I should spend my first Christmas without him this year. We've spent fifty years together. I've known your father all my life, but he's not sure about things this year. Please accept it, and I'll fill in for him," Mom Leneh told her daughter. "I'll spend one week with you all after Christmas before your father comes over for me. He will spend a night here before we leave. I hope that's fine with you all."

"Yes, Grandma. You're welcome to stay in my room," Nyenea replied.

"Thank you, my dear Nyenea," Ma Leneh said. Ma Leneh was glad to spend some time with her daughter and grandson. She wished she could steal more of their time while she was there. Her grandson was so much fun to be around.

• • •

The house was a bit noisy, and the dinner table was more crowded than usual. Everyone had something to say about the farm.

Mr. Mleh felt good inside. "We're glad to have everyone here today. It's our joy to have a family gathering, and we pray that God will give all of us long lives so that we can celebrate every year. We're glad to be fulfilling our dreams as a family. We always wanted to be away from the big towns and out here in the village where life is better. My father always said there's life in the village, and lives in the cities. We're glad to welcome all of you. Please feel free," Mr. Mleh told their guests.

After dinner that night, Mr. Mleh told his wife that Nyenea had confirmed his willingness to take over the farm when he grew up. "He's excited about the pigs, chickens, and crops. He said that he wants us to send the first eggs to his sisters in the United States. I'll be calling your brother after Christmas to confirm purchase of the farming machines and the girls' tuition fees. The machines will help a lot in clearing the fields and plowing the soil for planting."

The house awoke upon Christmas morning to the terrible news of a rebel attack from Ivory Coast on Botuwou, a border town between Liberia and Ivory Coast. The attack was on Christmas Eve, 1989, and was led by Charles Taylor, a former cabinet director for the General Services Agency (GSA) under President Samuel K. Doe.

"Charles Taylor is a notorious criminal who allegedly broke out of jail in Massachusetts in the United States," President Doe said. He had wanted Charles Taylor to be extradited to Liberia for stealing some money from the governent.

"We have had so many coups d'etats that no one can keep up with the number," Mr. Mleh said as he listened to Liberia Broadcasting System (LBS) shortwave radio on Christmas morning.

The news disturbed Mr. Mleh a bit, but he decided not to spoil the celebration. He told his wife, "It's just one of those many uprisings that we've been having, but the government said it ended yesterday when the AFL sent them back across the border into Ivory Coast." Mr. Mleh thought that the notion of trying to overthrow the government from the border was absurd. "It is always in Monrovia that the people try to unseat the government. Why in Nimba County? I'll ask my in-law, Kiamu, about it since he's in the United States. Maybe he knows more about it."

The Christmas party was fine, with lots of gifts for Nyenea from his sisters, his grandparents, his parents, and Dekie. Nyenea also bought a gift for Dekie. His mom had helped him to buy a pair of black college shoes for Dekie. Nyenea thanked everyone for his gifts and wrote a letter to his sisters in appreciation.

Dear sisters,

I am fine, as are Mom and Dad. We had a big Christmas party. I love the farm, and I wish you all were here. I miss you all a lot. Thanks for my gifts. I have a new friend called Dekie. He's a worker here on the farm. I wish you all a Merry Christmas and a happy new year.

Love,
Nyenea

"This is my best Christmas ever, Mama and Papa. Thanks for my gifts. I am very happy," Nyenea said.

"You are welcome," Mr. Mleh said to his son. "We're glad to be your parents, and you are very special to us."

On Christmas evening, Mr. Mleh tuned in to the BBC shortwave program *Focus on Africa* and heard the spokesman for the rebels speak about the attack and call for the resignation of President Samuel K. Doe.

"We are the National Patriotic Front of Liberia (NPFL). We'll take over Liberia and free our people, who have been suffering under the dictatorship of Doe," the spokesman said.

He started thinking about President Doe's first year in office. He had been seen by many Liberians as a true liberator from the oppressive rule of the former colonial leaders, the so-called Americo-Liberians who ruled for 120 years in deception and isolated the indigens.

President Doe, in one of his first written speeches to the nation, had said, "We are beginning the new government with much knowledge and experience about the great injustices suffered by the masses of our people. We are entering this new part of Liberian history with a song of those acts. The previous government has held our people down for too long. We seek to build a new society in which we have justice, human dignity, equal opportunities, and fair treatment for all."

On another occasion in 1980, he gave a heartwarming speech. "For too long did the masses of our people live in their own country, only to be treated like slaves on a plantation. For too long have our suffering people cried out for freedom, only to be put behind the bars of oppression. For nearly one hundred years, our people...were not considered as citizens under the laws of our country." These were welcome words to the deprived citizens, but the joy of the masses was short-lived when President Doe turned out to be a tyrant and the most feared dictator of his people.

Mr. Mleh got angry on hearing those remarks from the spokesman. "We don't need you to liberate us! You're all the same!" As a whole, the country was concerned, and the news was received with mixed reactions. Many simply didn't believe either the rebels or the government. The present government also claimed to liberate the natives from the Americo-Liberians who had ruled for 120 years, but it was the worst in human rights abuse and corruption, led by figureheads and sycophants who didn't care about its people. The news about the rebel attacks brought relief to tribes considered enemies of the government, such as the Gios and the Manos.

The guests at the house started leaving immediately after Christmas. Most of them were upset by the news. Mr. Mleh called his brother in-law in the United States and was shocked by what he said. "The NPFL rebels comprise some Americo-Liberians and other tribes living in the United States. I was approached by some of my friends, but I didn't consent to supporting the rebellion."

"But why didn't you inform me of this?" Mr. Mleh asked.

"I didn't think it was going to get this far, and I did not want to worry you and your family. But now that it has turned out this way, I think it's important that you get your family out as soon as possible," Kaimu said.

"How are our girls?" Mr. Mleh changed the topic. He didn't want to leave after investing much in the farm.

"They're fine and getting used to the harsh winter weather. We had a wonderful Christmas together," Kiamu noticed a change in his in-law's voice.

"We did the same here with your mother and few members of my family around. Did you by any chance share this news of this rebel attack with your father?"

"Yes, I did," Kiamu said.

"Well, your father refused to come here for Christmas." They talked about the farming equipment but Kiamu didn't want his brother in-law to invest immediately.

Mr. Mleh hung up after they chatted and left for the farm. "Your brother confirmed the news, but I want us to watch it for some time and see what's next," Mr. Mleh told his wife. He had decided not to frighten her with negative news. "Things will be fine, but let's wait and see."

A week later, the government of Liberia showed footage of captured rebels on TV. In January, the rebels announced the capture of Sanniquelle, the capital city of Nimba County. Again the government's spokesman denied the rebel claims and said that Liberia was free of rebels.

"I am Charles Ghankay Taylor, commander in chief of NPFL. I want Doe to leave power now, or I'll march to Monrovia in no time!" Taylor told the BBC's *Focus on Africa* program. By this time, the whole country was confused.

The rebel leader was president of the Liberians Association in America. He had led a delegation of his association to Liberia after waves and waves of riots started crippling the Liberian economy (the rice riots) in 1979. His delegation remained in the country until the overthrow of President Tolbert's government by Master Sergeant Samuel K. Doe. The rebel leader saw an opportunity of getting a share of the Liberian economy, so he decided to stay.

He maneuvered his way up and soon became the director of the General Services Agency, a cabinet post. He was responsible for bringing in all the latest cars for the bush boys, who were now leaders. He left the country for the United States later in 1983 and was accused by the president of embezzling huge sums of money. No one knew the real deal between the president and his minister because corruption was the order of the day in his government. With cash, Taylor started plans to remove his former boss, President Doe, from power. He took some young men from Nimba County to Libya for training with the help and support of Burkina Faso and Ivory Coast. From there, he launched his deadly assault on Liberia.

Mr. Mleh continued to work and watch the situation as every other Liberian did. The news about the rebels just did not go away, but Liberians got used to it and continued with their daily lives. He asked the workers to keep working and not be distracted by what "they" were saying. Liberia was a small country compared to others in West Africa, and news spread like wildfire, with everyone having their versions. The people soon forgot about the state radio and Liberian TV reports and turned to the BBC African Service for reliable information.

Dekie started worrying about his mother and younger sisters, Lulu and Zowahbah, in Sanniquelle. If the BBC reports were true, his folks were now in Sanniquelle. He had to travel there, but he didn't want to leave his newfound family. He had moved to the main house. He had his own room with a ceiling fan and a bathroom to himself. Mr. Mleh had taught him how to drive, so he drove the car out on errands. This was the first time in his life that he felt appreciated by others. He had always wanted to complete university and help his mom and sisters. However, he had only known suffering and hardships. His father had been a common laborer as a rubber tapper who was entitled to a mud hut with a single room and a porch. He and his sisters slept in the corridor. There was always hunger. He worried about his folks, and his eyes said it all.

One night, Polan called him in to discuss the situation. "Have you heard from your mom since Christmas?"

"No, Ma," Dekie answered.

"I want you to go there and see them. If there's anything that we can do, we'll help, but I want you go there and see them first," Polan said.

Dekie could not believe what she'd said to him. That same night, Nyenea had a horrible dream about Dekie. In his dream, Dekie became mean to him upon his return from Sanniquelle.

The next day in the morning, Nyenea went into Dekie's room. "Morning, Dekie. Mama said that you'll be traveling this morning."

"Yes, I am going to visit my mom and sisters in Sanniquelle."

"I've been keeping this for a long time. Please take it and use it to help you on your journey." Nyenea had kept the twenty-dollar bill that his sisters had given him at the airport. Nyenea also explained his dream to Dekie.

"That's just a dream. You're my friend, and friends we'll always be," Dekie said. Nyenea also gave Dekie some of the pictures they had taken together on Christmas Day.

"I told my sisters about you," Nyenea said.

"That was very kind of you. I hope to meet them one day."

Dekie thanked Mr. Mleh and the family for being kind to him. He said he would return soon. Polan and Nyenea dropped Dekie off in Kakata at the bus station. Polan gave him twenty dollars for transportation and his upkeep. "We'll be praying for you. Please take care of yourself and greet your mom and sisters."

They exchanged good-byes and left for the farm. Nyenea started crying as they drove off.

"He's not going to be away for long. Maybe for a week or two. He'll soon be with you," Polan had told her son. Nyenea explained his dream to his mom. Her first reaction was mixed, but she didn't show it. "Let's pray for Dekie's safe trip to Sanniquelle and back."

On the farm, Polan kept thinking about her son's dream. She had always listened to all of her children.

When they still lived in Bong Mines, Neneh had a dream one night about their housekeeper. In her dream, he had stolen some money and run away. A week later, the housekeeper stole $500 and ran away.

Whether it was a dream or not, Polan listened to what they said. She shared Nyenea's dream with her husband that night as they strolled toward the poultry.

"I don't want you to worry, my dear. Dekie can never harm Nyenea," Mr. Mleh said. They came across one of the guards on duty.

"How is everything tonight?" Mr. Mleh asked.

"We're OK, but we need some new batteries for our flashlights."

Mr. Mleh instantly thought of Dekie. "Well, Dekie will soon be back. But until then, you can always pick up new batteries every two days."

"Thanks, sir."

Dekie got to Gbarnga, Bong County, and met conflicting reports from the drivers. Some said they could not risk their lives and cars by going to Sanniquelle because the city was not safe, but other drivers said that it was safe. He spent the night in the bus station with other passengers. Late in the night, a few buses came from Sanniquelle with passengers. By dawn, all the buses started loading for Sanniquelle. There were hundreds of government soldiers and checkpoints along the road, checking cars as they passed by. Dekie counted more than a hundred checkpoints between Gbarnga and Sanniquelle, which was about thirty miles. Most of the people going to Sanniquelle were either checking on families or going to get them out.

Dekie found his sister Zowahbah at the bus station, trying to send him a letter. They greeted each other very emotionally with everyone staring in their direction.

"How are Mama and Lulu?"

"We've been so worried about you since this news started," Zowahbah said.

"But I've been worried also because we heard that the rebels took—"

"Shhh," Zowahbah put a finger over her lips. "We're not allowed to use the word *rebel* here but rather *freedom fighters*."

Dekie went blank on hearing that. He kept his thoughts to himself as he walked home with his sister without saying a word until they reached their house. He noticed the heavy presence of government soldiers in the city. There was harassment from government soldiers on the road to his house.

"A man walking alone was arrested and detained until he was identified by a well-known citizen. Most young men have lost their lives over the charges of being rebel supporters or for wearing the red T-shirts and blue jeans that the freedom fighters use as a uniform," Zowahbah informed her brother.

Dekie's mom was so glad to see him after a year. She started crying just as she did when he had decided to stay and work to complete his studies. They sat for a long time without a word.

"I'm happy to see you, my son. I wanted you to come and attend school here but you preferred BWI," Ma Yah said. "We received the last letter you wrote about your new family and friend, Nyenea. How're they?"

"They're fine, and they sent you everything in that bag," Dekie said. Polan had put laundry and bath soaps, dried fish, and all of her daughters' clothes and shoes for Dekie's sisters. Dekie's mom was shocked and speechless for few seconds before saying, "I thank my God."

Dekie gave her twenty dollars. "They said hi, and if things are not OK, we can live on their farm." Dekie thought about Nyenea and his family that night as he lay in bed.

Mleh prepared the land for a rice farm thrice as large as the previous one. He now awaited the arrival of the March or April rainy season to start planting rice. He had already planted cassava on the farm. The sugarcane had been harvested and taken to the factory for grinding. He contacted a sugar factory in Monrovia that agreed to buy the whole output. The sugar factory paid a good price, which encouraged him to plant a larger cane farm. They thanked God in church that Sunday for such an abundant harvest.

The news about the NPFL rebels became a topic on the lips of every Liberian. By March, the country was on a war footing, with claims of cities and towns falling to rebels. All the international media outlets had stories about Liberia every day. The Mleh family had not heard from Dekie for a week. Mr. Mleh felt his absence far more than he thought. There was no one to run errands, which gave him more work to do daily. Nyenea kept asking his mom whether Dekie was ever going to come back. He had no one to play with.

One night, the state TV broadcasted pictures of Sanniquelle under the control of the government forces. The family sat quietly as the reporter went from one street to the other, confirming the government's claims. The whole nation believed the government's claims because of the report. Mr. Mleh doubted everything he saw on the newscast but because of his wife's fears, he never said a word about it.

Dekie asked about his childhood friend, Saye, but he noticed something strange in the city. There were not many young men. Most of the men he saw were well into their sixties. He asked his sister Lulu about it on their way to check on his good friend Saye. Lulu was excited to go with her brother so she could meet with her secret lover Saye. It had been a long time since she last saw him. She had loved him as far back as when she was twelve years old. She had fallen down on on her way home from school. He had helped her up and taken her home. Lulu had been in love with him even after they'd moved to Gibi and returned recently, when she was sixteen. Lulu was older than Zowahbah and younger than Dekie.

"Many of the young men are disappearing. Every day we hear about someone who left home and was never seen again," Lulu said. The expression on Dekie's face was horror at what his sister revealed. He got so afraid that he wanted to leave the same day.

"Do the police know about this?" Dekie had asked.

His sister tried to change the topic, but it was too late. Their mother had warned them on the night of Dekie's arrival not to mention anything about the disappearance of young boys to him. Dekie's mom had decided not to frighten him.

His friend was in bed, pretending to be sick. His mother, Ma Kou, told them he had not come out of his room for a week. When Dekie entered the room, he saw that his friend was not sick. He was desperately afraid. They sat there for a while in silence.

"Have you been to the hospital?" Dekie asked.

Saye didn't know what to tell his friend—whether to lie or not. He was really happy to see Dekie, but he could not express his happiness in the presence of his mom and Lulu. "No, my mom bought me some tablets from her clinic." Being a nurse, his mother knew how to look after her son.

Saye and Dekie were agemates. Dekie and Saye had started school together as kids. They always saw each other as brothers. Their parents were close friends. Saye's father had died a year after Dekie's father. They had shared each other's sorrows and joys. He was also happy to see his friend, Lulu. Since she and her family had moved back, he saw that she was very beautiful, but he never said anything to her about it. He too kept her as his secret lover for fear of her mother and Dekie.

Saye was not sick, but he and his mom had faked his sickness to escape the forced recruitment of young boys aged ten years and up. All his age-mates had left for an unknown destination without the knowledge of their parents. Some parents actually knew what went on but didn't express opposition for fear of their lives, and others secretly supported the rebels. There were men visiting homes at night to seek support and sympathizers for the rebel movement. Because of the unpopularity of Doe's adminis-tration among the Gios and Manos, there was an instant support for the rebels in Nimba County, where both tribes lived.

Alone, Dekie visited Saye two days later. "Man, what's happening to the young men in this city?"

Saye took a long time to answer. He had known Dekie all his life, but it was difficult to trust others with the kind of situation unfolding in Sanniquelle and in the country. He had seen a family member betray another member to the government soldiers and that entire family was murdered. He decided to explain some things to his friend. "Why did you come here, man? This city is about to explode."

"LBS, the state radio station, said that the city was under the govern-ment's control, and I can see government soldiers all over," Dekie answered.

Saye told his friend everything going on in the city. "Most boys are signing up to join the rebels in an unknown destination. They've been here on several occasions to get me, and that's why I faked this sickness to deceive them until I can leave. Man, I'm not going anywhere. We should leave tomorrow, or we'll be forced into their ranks."

"But my mom didn't mention this to me. Anyway, I'll leave with you tomorrow," Dekie said.

On his way back home, he planned to discuss his trip with his mom, but as soon as he got home, his mom approached him on the topic.

"You have to leave tonight, or things may get bad for us. There were some men here to take you for training with NPFL rebels tonight. If you refuse, they'll kill us. But I'm willing to die if that be the case," his mom said firmly.

Dekie's heart pounded. His sisters were crying as their mother tried to calm them down.

"You have to leave this city tonight, Dekie. Your father would never agree to such a thing." Ma Yah fought back her tears. She hated everything about the rebels and didn't want her children to get involved.

The rebels were quite small in number. Therefore, they resorted to a compulsory recruitment in captured towns and villages. They had already surrounded the town of Sanniquelle for more than a week. The first time they fought for the city, they were driven back and later retreated. They suffered more casualties than the government forces. The rebels quickly adopted a hit-and-run technique that usually caught the government soldiers off guard. The government soldiers also suffered from deserters and lack of morale as the Krahn soldiers were treated better than their fellow soldiers. The war started taking on a different nature as members of the Gios and Manos ethnic groups were hunted and beheaded for presumably supporting the rebels. The rebels had planned to take Sanniquelle the next day as the last government stronghold in Nimba County.

There was a curfew from 7:00 p.m. to 7:00 a.m. in Sanniquelle, which made it difficult for anyone to travel at night. Dekie tried to think of a way out, but he could not come up with anything concrete. At eight o'clock, a knock was heard on their door. The house went quiet for a long time without anyone moving. Most often, a knock on your door meant danger for the entire house. At times, the government soldiers took the men for interrogation; they were never seen again. Or the rebels forcibly recruited them.

"It's me, Saye," Saye said in a very low voice. When Dekie heard Saye's voice at the door, he attempted to opened it, but his mom refused, saying that it was a trick. But Dekie was sure that he heard his friend's voice. "No, Mom, it's Saye at the door," he whispered. He slowly opened the door and saw his friend standing there, breathless, with a small backpack.

"I ran away from them, but they may just come here to get us. Let's not spend the night in this city! We cannot throw our lives away," Saye managed to say breathlessly. He suggested that they go to a soldier friend to spend the night and then leave early the next morning. Dekie packed a few clothes and put them into Saye's bag. Dekie's mom said a little prayer for them before they left. However, when they opened the door, there were three men in military uniforms standing there.

• • •

Meanwhile, Mr. Mleh and his family went not far from the farm in Kakata to call the girls. Nyenea had a very long discussion with his sisters. They were all in the university and were studying hard.

"We love you, Nyenea. Please study hard and be a nice boy to our parents!" Seanee said.

Nyenea talked to all of them for almost an hour.

Mr. Mleh's brother-in-law was adamant about him getting his family out of Liberia. "Look, inlaw! I'll help you to get everyone over. I read a report yesterday from the US State Department that left me very disturbed. The rebels are killing innocent civilians, and the government is also carrying out reprisal attacks on the Gios and Manos and against anyone who is sympathetic to the rebels," Kiamu said.

The adults drove back in silence, but Nyenea was excited and kept narrating his conversation with his sisters to his parents. Mr. Mleh was disturbed, and his wife knew it. She knew her husband so well that he could not hide his feeling from her.

After almost an hour, Polan broke the silence. "My brother wants to take our parents to the United States in April." They drove for another half an hour in silence before her husband looked in her direction. He and Kiamu had agreed to keep a low profile on discussions that had to do with state security. Polan could easily break down on hearing such news. The thought of leaving his farm to travel to the United States did not make any sense to him. He had invested more than $100,000 on the farm. To walk away was inconceivable.

"He told me to get new passports for your parents," Mr. Mleh answered his wife. She knew that he was hiding something from her but she decided to leave it at that. She felt sorry for her husband. Everytime she saw that look on his face, it meant he had a lot on his mind.

CNN was interviewing the rebel representative in the United States when they got home. "We'll take Sanniquelle in a day or two. Our freedom fighters have not killed civilians. Our fighters are well disciplined and will not harm them. After all, we are there to liberate them!"

Mr. Mleh walked away in anger to the mill with his son. "The so-called representative is a thief. Why does he call his thugs freedom fighters? They're killers and rapists." He fought hard not to let his son see the frustration on his face.

"Daddy, when will the chickens start laying eggs?" Nyenea asked his father as they passed the poultry.

"In two months. Then you can send some to your sisters," Mr. Mleh said, smiling at his son. "I want to talk to you about the news on the radio and TV."

"About Charles Taylor?" Nyenea asked.

His father was surprised to hear his son mention the rebel leader's name. "Where did you learn that?"

"Dekie told me that his name is Charles Ghankay Taylor," Nyenea replied.

"Well, I want you to stay out of any discussion with the workers that has to do with that name."

"Yes, Papa," Nyenea replied.

As they walked, he explained to his son the situation and how he was going to protect him and his mom. "Don't go off alone on the farm. Always ask permission from one of us. Just be careful from now on," Mr. Mleh warned his son.

CHAPTER 2

• • •

DEKIE AND SAYE WERE LED behind the house without a word. They were afraid because they didn't know their kidnappers or where they were heading. They quickly entered a rubber bush that led them to a shortcut beyond the city. This was strange territory to both of them. The three men led them to another four men who were also in military uniforms. The rebels used the tactic of using government soldiers' uniforms in most of their operations. They were surprised to see in the AFL uniform, but the four men didn't say a word to them along the way into the bush.

They didn't see any weapon on their kidnappers but later, the kidnappers picked up a bag along the road. The bag contained seven brand-new AK-47 rifles. Instantly, Dekie and Saye feared that their kidnappers were going to kill them. Saye decided to run away as soon as he got the chance. They walked in the forest for more than an hour before one of the men said, "You'll be treated well if you obey our commands! We'll not rest until we reach our destination. If you try to run, you'll be shot dead!"

Dekie's mom cried until no tears came out of her eyes. "Why did this happen to me? My son just came to see us, and he's now going to die," Ma Yah said. Her daughters sat quietly in the dark, sobbing, unable to comfort one another. "If you want to overthrow President Doe, why take my son? Will I ever see him again?" she lamented. She knew many mothers who were in the same situation and had never thought it could happen to her because her son was not living in the rebel-held territory. But now that it had happened, it only inflamed her hatred for the rebels.

Saye's mom, Kou, didn't worry much. She thought that her son was safe at Ma Yah's house with his friend. Saye had escaped from her house for him and Dekie to leave for Gbarnga that night or early the next morning.

"I'll check Ma Yah's house tomorrow morning," she said to herself before going to bed that night. She hated the day that some members of her Gio ethnic group came to tell her about the revolution and how everyone had a part to play.

"This is our struggle to liberate our people from the dictatorial regime of Samuel Doe," the men had said. Because of the sympathy among some Nimbalians, the NPFL rebels used their county as a front line and a support base to oust President Doe. The rebels' secret recruitment team went from house to house to persuade citizens of Nimba to their cause. Saye's mom refused outright to allow anyone take her son away.

Polan decided to talk to her brother about her husband's attitude. She went to Kakata to call Kiamu. They discussed the crisis unfolding daily on various US news networks. Kiamu tried to hide his discussion with his brother-in-law from his sister, but he decided to tell his sister, thinking she could persuade her husband to leave the country.

"I told your husband to get you all out of the country before it's too late," Kiamu said. "Things are going to get bad in Liberia. I think you should get out while you can."

There was a long silence from Polan. Words refused to come out of her mouth. "What's going to happen to our farm?" she finally asked.

"You can always get another farm when the war is over, sister, but for now you have got to get out! I visited a family friend who arrived yesterday from Yekepa in Nimba County, and his account of the situation is gruesome! Please talk to your husband. I'll help to get you all out."

Polan could hardly speak. She barely managed to tell him good-bye.

Kiamu met the girls that evening. They had begun to worry about their parents back home and planned to tell their parents to leave Liberia. They had read and watched news on the Liberian crisis. Kiamu made it clear that the war in Liberia might take between five and fifteen years, depending on the strength of the Liberian government. "After the independence of some African countries in the late fifties and early sixties, they got into civil wars that are yet to end. Angola, Sudan, and Uganda are still at war among themselves, for example. There has never been a short civil war. This is not a military coup that will only last for days and then be over."

The girls were silent as he gave them a bit of African history.

Seanee spoke out. "What was their response when you talked to them?"

"They're not willing to leave after investing heavily in the farm. I want you all to appeal to them about the dangers of the war. The rebels may be faraway from them for now, but they're moving toward the capital city, Monrovia. This will cover Gibi where your folks live," Kiamu answered.

The girls stared at one another. "We've got to convince them to get out of Liberia!" Neneh said. They agreed and thanked their uncle for his concern.

● ● ●

It was a very dark path. The torchlight was only used when they met the four men and then it wasn't used again. It was so dark that one could not see the ground or the palms of his hands. You could not see the other person's figure in the darkness. Saye had planned to run off by asking for permission to use the toilet. He decided that if he was allowed to go into the bush, he would escape but he was afraid to speak to his kidnappers.

"Excuse me, sirs. I…want to use the toilet," Saye said.

"OK," said one of the men, "take one step off the road and do it!" They all stood there. After he took a step, two of the men surrounded him with one in the front and one at the back.

"You have a minute, and then we'll leave!" the same man said. Dekie thought of how his friend had been adamant about not joining a bunch of thieves and thugs. *I hope he's not trying to run off. This may not be the best chance for now.* He had thought about escaping too but decided against it when he saw that the situation and the timing weren't right. It was too dark, and he didn't know where to run. *Where will I go in this deep forest? These guys may use their guns without remorse. I'll live for now and escape one day.*

Saye squatted between the men and pretended that he was defecating. Just then, an owl flew past them, shook the bush, and made a loud noise with its wings. As the men turned to look, Saye saw his chance of escape. He knocked down one of the men and took off. They all turned and shot randomly into every direction. The guns were deafening, and he saw red flashes. There was a loud scream from Saye. Within two minutes, the drama ended. Two of the men returned from the chase. The forest was dark and silent as the two figures emerged with a dimmed torchlight. They didn't know which way Saye had run but they tried.

The leader asked, "Did you kill him?"

"Yes, sir, but we didn't find his body," one of them answered.

Dekie heard his heart beating hard. He tried to control himself, but he could not believe what he'd just witnessed. His friend was dead, and he was now alone with these murderers. He had to be careful now, or they might well kill him too. He thought of how he had run away during a student demonstration when the government soldiers stormed their school in search of some students at BWI. He had gone under his bed and remained there until the campus was clear. But this was his first real experience with gunfire at such close range. He could still hear his friend's voice in his head. "I'll avenge my friend on these dogs one day!" He started crying but pretended before his kidnappers.

"Your friend just died, and we'll do the same to you if you say a word! From now on, we'll do the talking. No more breaks until we reach our destination," the assumed leader said and shoved him from the back, almost knocking him off his feet. Later, they heard a loud burst of gunshots in the distance.

● ● ●

Mr. Mleh was listening to Voice of America's *Daybreak Africa program* at 6:30 a.m. when he heard the rebels' spokesman claiming the success of the NPFL's takeover of the city of Sanniquelle.

"We took the city without a fight," the spokesman said.

His mind went straight to Dekie and his family. There were lots of questions on his mind. *Why is he staying longer when he knows that Sanniquelle is a front line?*

He blamed himself for sending Dekie into such a dangerous war zone. "We may never see him again." Mr. Mleh had heard the rumors about rebels recruiting young men to fight their senseless war. Since the day he met Dekie when he was looking for workers, he had known the boy was a resilient young man. At almost six feet tall, Dekie stood out among his friends. His family had decided to adopt Dekie when he returned from Sanniquelle. He thought of how Nyenea had taken to Dekie. Nyenea was lonely, and it was obvious. He constantly asked if Dekie was coming back. With the fall of Sanniquelle, Gbarnga was next in line of cities to go to the rebels. Mr. Mleh started giving some thought to his brother-in-law's advice. *If the rebels take over our farm, what will become of us? Will we become their slaves, or will they kill us all?* He would talk to his wife before going to work that morning.

• • •

Ma Yah and her daughters fell asleep and were awakened by heavy gunfire that lasted for almost two hours. The rebels surrounded the town and came from every direction, attacking the government soldiers. They took over the road leading to and from the city. Most soldiers who tried to escape were caught and killed. It started at 5:30 a.m., and by 7:30 a.m. the operation ended. The city was under their control. They went on a house-to-house search and rounded up all the progovernment supporters and officials and killed them.

Ma Yah and her girls stayed indoors just as they had done the first time the rebels took over the city. By eight o'clock, they heard men speaking in their native tongue, Gio, asking everyone to come out and go about their normal business.

"You're free from the tyranny of Doe! If you have a soldier in your house, report him now, or we'll kill you and the soldier! Starting today, there's no more curfew."

In less than a minute after the men spoke, there were shouts from every quarter of the city. People came out in jubilation, congratulating the rebels. Ma Yah cautioned her daughters against taking part in any activities under the rebels and to keep away from the streets. "I've lost my only son, and I don't want to suffer again." The girls sat silently, listening to their mom.

Ma Kou ran to her friend's house to find out about her son. The door was closed. She was about to turn back when the door opened. Zowahbah came out, looking around. Ma Kou called out just before she could step back inside. Zowahbah opened the door, and Ma Kou entered. On getting into the house, she met her friend, Ma Yah, seated and crying in a hoarse voice.

Fear swept over her when she saw her friend crying.

"They took away our children last night," Ma Yah managed to say. Ma Kou broke down in tears on hearing the news. "Why us? Can't they fight without using our children? My son is not well and can't survive in the bush. He's an asthmatic." They spent the next hour in silence.

● ● ●

Saye got shot in the lower back and thigh. The sounds of the AK-47s confused him, and for a moment, he thought he was dead. The bullet ripped some flesh from his thigh, but after he noticed that his leg was not broken, he kept on running and falling as he stumbled and smashed against trees and ropes. He heard the bullets ripping the leaves and cutting off tree branches as he ran. He stopped after an hour when there was no other sound but himself and inspected his wounds. The forest was quiet and calm as he sat down under a large tree. He felt the tree and and noticed that it was wet.

"Oh God! Please help me!" He felt like ending his life. Every sound startled him as he sat in total darkness. He tried to go over the whole scenario, but he noticed that he was bleeding profusely and his mind wasn't working properly. He felt ashamed of leaving his friend alone with those murderers, "If they kill him, I'll never forgive myself. I should have stayed and planned our escape together."

The pain in his back was so excruciating that he could not sit straight. He tore off a piece of cloth from his pants to bandage his wound. After that was done, the blood stopped flowing from his thigh, but his back was wet with his blood. He didn't know his whereabouts, and he could not find a road or path that would lead him to a town or village. They walked for more than five hours from Sanniquelle before his escape.

He stood up and tried to keep going, but he realized that he could not walk anymore. He thought he saw a light normally used by hunters, but his vision clouded and he fell down, unable to move his legs. He passed out.

After walking all night, Dekie and his kidnapper reached a small village containing three huts. There was no sign of the village's inhabitants but he saw a girl of about twelve years old seated by a fire, heating water. They were greeted by a middle-aged man wearing a wig. "We were unable to bring Saye, but we have a replacement. I think they've cleared the entire city of all young men, sir!" the leader reported. Dekie could not believe what he heard. *The commanders sent men to town to get people for their personal recruitment. The government is propagating lies while the rest of the country is becoming a land for desperadoes*, Dekie thought.

Dekie was led to the kitchen where the girl sat by the rebel wearing a wig. "My name is Colonel Zokaya. They call me Mosquito. We want you to feel free. Tomorrow, we'll reach our base in Botuwou, but you need to rest because you will need those legs for a day's walk. We're going to train you as a guerilla fighter to liberate your country from the dictator Doe! From today's date, you're a freedom fighter!" Mosquito tried to show some kindness to Dekie in order to gain his confidence, but Dekie remained stiff.

"What's your name?" Mosquito asked.

"Dekie," Dekie answered. Mosquito noticed that Dekie had been to school and spoke better English than all his boys. *I'll have him as my personal bodyguard*, he thought.

Mosquito called the girl and instructed her to feed his guest with enough food. Dekie never saw his kidnappers again after they had reported to Mosquito. Later, he saw five young men coming toward him from the bush. They carried bananas, pineapples, and a fifty-pound bag of rice. Their hair looked as if it had not seen water and razor for months, and they smelled as if water was taboo.

They spoke in Mano as they reported to Mosquito. The boys were between the ages of twelve and fifteen and were barefoot. They greeted him respectfully and sat in a circle by the fire to warm themselves. It occurred to Dekie that he was the best-dressed guy in the village as his food was handed to him by the girl. The bowl and cup were clean, and that surprised him. The girl gave him bananas and sliced pineapple. He ate half of it and gave the rest back to the girl who sat by, staring at him along with the boys.

Dekie thought about his mom and the Mleh family. He had missed Nyenea so much since he left Gibi. His thoughts were interrupted when the boys mentioned the capture of Sanniquelle the night before. One of them said that NPFL now controlled Nimba County now that its last city had fallen. Dekie choked as his throat went dry, and he drank the cup of water he held in one swallow. *What's going to happen to my mom and sisters? Will I see them again? What will I tell Saye's mom?* For a moment, he didn't know where he was.

Col. Mosquito had stood over him for a minute, trying to get his attention without success. "Dekie!" Dekie jumped to his feet and almost fell.

"Are you all right?" Col. Mosquito asked.

"Yes, but I'm tired from the journey," Dekie lied.

"You may go in and rest. Why didn't you tell me that you wanted to sleep?" Col. Mosquito asked Dekie if he wanted a bit of the local drink, cane juice, or some weed to help him ease his pains. Dekie said no and left for the room. The girl showed him a piece of mat and walked out. He looked around and saw lots of looted goods lying around on the dirt floor. His kidnappers' uniforms were hung along with military boots. It seems that his captors had raided nearby villages for everything. He tried to go over what happened the night before, but he fell asleep as soon as his head hit the mat.

● ● ●

"My dear Polan, the rebels took Sanniquelle this morning. I want us to keep it a secret from Nyenea. He may not be able to assimilate the news," Mr. Mleh said.

Polan stood in shock, staring at her husband. "What shall we do as they get closer to Gibi?"

"I met our pastor yesterday. He thinks that they can be contained for some time before they get farther. He believes that the government will not allow a certain portion of the country to fall into rebel hands."

Polan's face said it all. Mr. Mleh knew that it was time to discuss the matter but for some reason, he held back.

"Did you and my brother discuss anything else besides the machines?"

The question was a shock to him, and it took some time to respond. He could not face his wife at this time.

"I want our family to go through this together. You don't have to carry the burden alone. I know you're the head, but we should work things out together," Polan continued.

Mr. Mleh knew that her trip yesterday had something to do with this. "Kiamu wants us to leave the country," he said finally. There was a long silence as they stood apart, staring at each other. Polan reached out and hugged him. "We should decide now, darling."

"Let's see what happens in two months," he said. Her brother had said that they should leave Liberia in two weeks, but she didn't want her brother to come between them, although she knew he meant well for them.

"Is two months not too long?" Many Liberians thought like Mr. Mleh. They believed that this crisis would end soon. Others held the opposite view. Some Liberians had started leaving the country for her West African neighbors. People with enough money started leaving for the United States and some European countries. Mr. Mleh thought for a long time and said no. He knew it was not the best answer, but he had to find a way out this time.

● ● ●

He saw birds flying over him peacefully. One of the birds called out to him, but he smiled. "I have no wings to fly," Saye said.

"We can take you to a place where no man will ever bother you again." They took him up into the sky and showed him the beauty of earth from the sky.

"Is it always like this from here?" Saye asked. The wind was calm and peaceful, and he felt the cold wet cloth upon his face. Saye had been dreaming.

"Oh, you're up, son," he heard the voice of a woman as she wiped the sweat off his face with a damp cloth. He opened his eyes to see her sitting next to him on a mat.

"Hello, you've been talking in your sleep for some time now. My name is Ma Norn. My husband found you in the forest last night when he was hunting."

"Thank you, Ma," he managed to say. He tried to turn around to see his surroundings, but the pain in his back prevented him. Ma Norn told him to lie down until her husband returned. Saye tried to take a good look at the woman, but his eyes closed slowly, and he went back to sleep.

Quianue had been hunting for more than twenty-five years, but this was a new experience. At first, he thought he saw the bush hog he'd shot earlier. He took aim but just when he was about to shoot, the object had fallen to the ground. He lowered his gun and turned his headlight toward the object. He stopped in his tracks when he saw a young boy lying in blood. At first, he thought the boy was a wizard who had changed into human form after being shot, but the boy's clothes were like those from the city. He decided to take him home.

Back at the house, his wife thought her husband had killed a big animal, so she hurried out of bed and turned up the lantern. "Oh, my dear! I'm coming to help you!" Ma Norn said. She was shocked to find her husband with a young boy lying on the floor. At first, she thought her husband had shot the boy. She lowered her voice and said, "I'm so sorry. How did it happen?"

"Let's get him cleaned up and try to stop him from bleeding to death," Quianue said and quickly added that he didn't shoot him.

"Let's not let our neighbors know about him," Quianue told his wife. At seven the next morning, Quianue left for a nearby town to seek the assistance of a native doctor. He tried to figure out why he was saving another person's life when he could not save his only son, Yeanue, who had been taken away by unknown gunmen.

Yeanue had been taken away a month before by Mosquito and his men. Since then, his parents had not heard anything about his whereabouts or seen his kidnappers. Ma Norn sat by Saye, looking at his face, and imagined her only son. Yeanue was fifteen, a tenth grade student at LASS High School in Yekapa. He had escaped from the recruitment team to hide in his village of Tepo. He wanted to complete school one day and help his parents.

Ma Norn wondered whether their patient would survive. *Who is this boy? Oh God, please help us! Our country is on the verge of collapse with strange and bad people hovering over our towns and villages.*

● ● ●

Dekie and his new commander got along very well. As soon as Dekie woke up, Mosquito called him for a briefing. Dekie made up his mind to give in and work with them. *If you can't beat them, join them.* He got to know all of them by names and ranks.

Col. Mosquito told him of his training in Ivory Coast two years back. He had been a graduate of the BWI accelerated program where he earned an associate degree as an auto mechanic in 1985. Dekie was happy to meet a former graduate of his school.

"I am a student at BWI too," Dekie said.

Mosquito smiled and called his boys around to congratulate Dekie. "You are my most educated soldier, and you will be assigned directly to me!"

The other guys saluted Dekie and welcomed him, but from then on, they didn't like him. Mosquito cautioned Dekie about his boys and advised him not to get too close to them. Dekie felt better for the first time that evening before their trip. They had to travel by night to avoid any hostile attacks from the pockets of leftover government soldiers. Col. Mosquito informed his men that they would leave at sunset. Everything was packed and ready when the first group of boys left with the loads fitted for a truck. The girl was asked to stay behind and walk with Mosquito. The journey was long and tiring. They walked for six hours before resting for thirty minutes in an abandoned farm kitchen.

They reached Botuwou at dawn, and Col. Mosquito asked Dekie to stay with him. The border town was small but packed with lots of men, old and young, wearing uniform red T-shirts and blue jeans. Dekie was shocked to see so many young boys and girls carrying guns. Others had sticks and machetes. There were looted cars coming from Sanniquelle and crossing the border into Ivory Coast. No one was idle. It seemed like no one cared about what they wore or how they looked. They were filthy with strong sweaty smells that followed them. Captured military trucks were parked. There was jubilation over the capture of Sanniquelle. Col. Mosquito went to his training commander to make his reports. After that, he introduced Dekie to his commander. "I have a decent recruit for you, sir. He's a student of BWI, my former school."

"BWI? What were you doing in Nimba? Have we captured Kakata already?" Gen. Dudu asked.

"I came to see my mom in Sanniquelle," Dekie said. Gen. Dudu was one of the trained soldiers from Libya. He looked mean and tough, and there was nothing cool about him. He didn't look like a normal human being. "You'll stay with Mosquito throughout the training. We want young guys like you to carry on the struggle for our country. We'll make you one of our best freedom fighters."

Mosquito had trained under Dudu in Ivory Coast. He was his commander and friend. Dudu depended on Mosquito for all his paper work because he could not recognize the letter A even if it was written as big as a three-story building. Normally, fighters brought in for the first time were not introduced to their commanders, but Mosquito had a special interest in Dekie, and he wanted him in the top ranks of the movement.

Mosquito took Dekie and the small girl to his house. There were rumors about the president, the Iron Lady, and the field commander coming to visit Sanniquelle. Dekie thought of President Samuel Doe coming to Sanniquelle. He got excited but his excitement was short-lived when Mosquito said that President Taylor was due in the next day. The six-week training was to commence that day but because of the visit of the rebel leader, it was postponed till the next day. Dekie saw the excitement on the faces of the small boys and thought of Nyenea and his family.

"How can this be happening when they should be in school?" Dekie said to himself. These boys were as young as eight years old. He was looking around for familiar faces when Mosquito called him.

● ● ●

The birds came again to take him away from the terrors and pains of this world. They took him behind the clouds where he only saw sunshine and experienced tranquility.

"Oh, I'm glad to be here again," Saye said. "We have a friend who can heal your back pain," said one of the birds. They flew higher and higher and met a very

beautiful bird with many colors. The bird touched his back with one of its feathers and the pains stopped at once.

Saye woke up and felt a cloth on his back. He had been dreaming again. He tried to speak but there was no strength in him. He was weak and soaked with sweat.

"Relax, son. We just got one of the bullets out of your back. You've been sleeping since yesterday afternoon. The native doctor advised that we give you some food so that you can regain your strength." Quianue said.

"Thank God! You're alive," Ma Norn said as she cleaned him up.

Quianue thanked the native doctor and paid him. He gave him some dried bush meat also. As a hunter, it was always expected of you to have some bush meat. He escorted him out of the village. He had known this man all his life, and the surrounding towns and villages respected him. He had a special gift as a native doctor. He healed 95 percent of his patients, or he asked that they be taken to a modern hospital if he could not restore their health. "Whose son is that boy?" the native doctor asked.

"I really don't know. I found him last night in the forest, half-dead," Quianue replied.

"There are strange men taking our children away at night. My son and some of our neighbors' boys were taken three weeks ago. Maybe that boy escaped from some of them and got shot in the process," the native doctor said.

"We hope he comes through and tells us what happened. We've not seen Yeanue since he was taken," Quianue said.

On his return, his wife was trying to spoon-feed Saye eddoes soup. He was responding but found it difficult to swallow and sit up at the same time.

"How's he doing?" Quianue asked.

"I think he's OK, but he's too weak from the loss of blood," Ma Norn told her husband.

Saye could not eat any more. He fell backward and felt a sharp pain in his back.

"Lie on your stomach for now, Saye," Ma Norn instructed.

"Oh, you already know his name," Quianue said.

"He called his name and another name—Dekie or something. He's been calling that name for some time now. I think he's calling for someone," Ma Norn said.

"Let's leave him alone for now. God willing, he will come through, and we'll get to know him better," Quianue said.

• • •

Mr. Mleh had serious misgivings about leaving his farm and Liberia for the United States. He believed there was no reason for him to hurry. Nyenea had been asking him about Dekie almost every day. He never had a concrete answer to give his son. He decided to tell him the truth.

"My son, Dekie may not come back until the war is over. The city he traveled to has been taken over by the rebels." Nyenea remained silent for a long time before tears slowly poured down his cheeks. "We may see him when the crisis ends."

Polan found it difficult to comfort her son. She had told her husband to decide about their future before it was too late. "It happened to Dekie. We may be next, and our children will not know where we are."

She spent lots of time watching CNN news. The footage from Sanniquelle was not good. Men ran around, wearing wigs and red T-shirts. They sang and danced to Lucky Dube's song "Freedom." She finally gave up trying to convince her husband. *Maybe, as our head, he's doing the right thing.* But Polan knew within herself that he wasn't right and that it was going to get worse soon. However, she just kept praying for her husband to change his mind soon.

• • •

The rebel leader was a small red-faced man. He was dressed in military camouflage with a bulletproof jacket. There was a huge applause from his fighters as he addressed them. He was flanked by his field commander, a spokesman, and a light-skinned short woman, known as the Iron Lady, wearing a red beret. There was applause for each word spoken by the leader. Dekie was stunned as he watched a different world unfold before his eyes. A few days ago, he was living in a rational world but here, he was looking at the most dreaded and dangerous rebel leader in Africa. *I wish Mr. Mleh could see this,* he thought. The rebel leader's convoy left an hour later with lots of armed men in captured government trucks at the front and back. The leader's car was between the guards. Dekie was still breathless when he heard a voice behind him.

"Col. Mosquito wants to see you immediately," a young boy about fifteen said to Dekie. The boy led the way to their commander's house through the crowd that still stood around.

Dekie noticed that his escort spoke decent English. "What's your name?"

"My name is Yeanue," Yeanue said."

Dekie wanted to know more about the boy and befriend him. "How long have you been here?"

"Six weeks. We'll be graduating this week." Yeanue felt free talking to Dekie.

"My name is Dekie. I'm from Gibi, and I was visiting my mom when they picked me and my friend up two days ago. I'm a senior student at BWI."

Instantly, the boy's eyes widened when he heard that Dekie was also a student. "I am a tenth-grade student from LASS High in Yekapa." They became friends and went on talking until they met Mosquito.

As early as four o'clock the next morning they went jogging as the training began. They jogged for miles, chanting war-like songs like "Anybody Say You Don't Like Ghankay, We Go Kill You like a Dog" for inspiration. For the first three weeks of training, it was all about shooting and physical exercises to make them fit and strong. Dekie got more prepared daily as he was interested in the shooting maneuvers. He became the best sharpshooter on base, and no one could stand against him in physical combat. He did the training as if he was a born soldier.

Mosquito kept taking Dekie aside for extra training. He gave him hard drugs. He wanted him to be the best sharpshooter in the rebel movement. "How's it?" he would ask Dekie after tying his arm and injecting him with the drugs. Sweat and strange feelings overtook Dekie's body every time he took cocaine.

"I'm fine, CO," Dekie would answer in a distant tone.

After a while, he saw himself as one of them and went for everything with his whole heart—something that pleased Mosquito.

Yeanue completed his training and was posted to the next attack on Gbarnga. He explained everything about himself to Dekie, and he asked Dekie to be his big brother. They became so close that they ate and slept together on the dirt floor. Yeanue and Dekie made a promise to try to protect each other and find their parents in case one of them died.

Dekie told him about himself. Dekie told him one day about Saye and how he was killed that night. Yeanue was sorry to hear about Saye, so he tried to encourage his new friend, Dekie. Yeanue didn't want to leave Dekie, but he had to leave the next day for Gbarnga.

"Big brother, I don't want to stay on the base. I want to go back to my parents and continue my education," Yeanue said. He remembered seeing the first ten members of his troop died during the initiation performed by a witch doctor. They were given a talisman meant to protect one from bullet but all of the boys that underwent the test died.

"Just be calm. I'll look for you as soon as I come to Gbarnga," Dekie promised. After Yeanue left, Dekie felt that he had lost him just like he had lost Saye.

● ● ●

Meanwhile, Saye kept calling for Dekie to come for him, but Dekie stood across the river, crying for his friend. "Dekie, Dekie, please come for me."

"I can't cross over to you," Dekie said.

Saye opened his eyes and saw Ma Norn seated by his mat. He was dreaming again.

"Saye, you're up."

Saye was much better after three weeks of rest. He had been dreaming a lot about Dekie. The pain in his back was already subsiding. He explained his ordeal to Quianue and his wife. Ma Norn asked him to stay with them a little while until the situation got better. Saye was recuperating fast. His new family was proud to see his ability to drink his herbs and eat.

"Where do you think they took your friend that night?" Quianue asked.

"I really don't know. We never knew where they were taking us, but I'm ashamed to say that I escaped without my friend. I'll not join their rebel group. I'm willing to die for my belief!" Saye said. Saye was strong enough to bathe himself and use the toilet. He also ate and walked around the hut at night. Up to this time, not many people in the village knew about him. Mr. Quianue and his wife kept him indoors all day.

● ● ●

The field commander and his men surrounded Gbarnga and cut off all routes to the city. By April, the city fell to NPFL rebels with ease. Camp Nama, the military base in Gbamga surrendered without a single shot. The rebels now controlled a large chunk of the country. The rebel leader declared himself president of Liberia right after the capture, claiming that he would take the rest of the country if President Samuel Doe did not resign and leave the country. To continue fighting their way forward, they recruited many boys and girls of any age. The young fighters were enticed with looted goods and marijuana and anything that numbed their bodies and minds. There were wizards to protect the fighters from bullets. It was called Zaykay. As long as you were marked on the forearm with the talisman, you were seen as being immune to any gunshot.

The country's economy collapsed as big companies like Liberian American Mining Company (LAMCO) and others shut down and their expatriates left Liberia. LAMCO was one of the largest iron-ore mining companies in Liberia, and it was located in Nimba County. All the schools in those areas were closed permanently. With the taking of Gbarnga, many people who could afford to leave the country left for peaceful countries so that their children could continue their education. The rebels never had enough sophisticated weapons to take the towns and cities. They mainly used Russian-made guns like AK-47s, Berettas, and pistols that were supplied by Libya through Burkina Faso and Ivory Coast to Liberia. The term "small soldier" was heard on many lips in the rebels' territory. There were kids as young as nine and ten carrying guns for the rebels.

Mr. Mleh thought about their future on the farm. In just a short time, there was large support among many Liberians for the rebels. The BBC shortwave program *Focus on Africa* soon became a popular program for all. Most people listened only to hear the voice of the rebel leader. He instantly became so popular that a two-year-old child could be heard calling his name. Some said, "Tailor, come and sew our clothes." Because Liberia was a small country with an illiteracy rate of more than 75 percent, it was easy for the rebels to gain popularity. The people would fall for anything. The national army became a place for armed robbers and uneducated young men. In the mideighties, President Doe called for boys as young as fifteen to join the army and of course, his call was heeded by many boys who were satisfied to be paid monthly and be used as instruments to carry out the commands of the president. As the government lost territories to the rebels, the president said, "The rebels are not coming for me alone but for the whole country." It was hard to believe, but it proved to be true, and many Liberians started leaving their homes for displaced centers.

Mr. Mleh decided that his family would leave the country in June. He had listened to their pastor and believed him over his wife. Polan tried her best to convince him to leave earlier, but he insisted that if things didn't improve by May, they would leave in June. News on Liberia was no longer encouraging. The government's ELBC radio spread propaganda about their army still being in control of every rebel-controlled territory. He got so worked up about the news in the country that it could be seen in his eyes. He had just gotten a big contract to supply Bong Town supermarket with chickens and eggs in June. This was his first major break since they moved to the farm. "I hope all the rebels and their leaders will one day rot in jail for what they've done to our nation!"

● ● ●

Dekie completed his training in style. For the last three weeks of infantry training in the jungle, he was the first to pass. Their commander, Gen. Dudu, put up a challenge to Dekie. He knew that the boy was nowhere close to his caliber as a trained rebel from the mountains of Libya. "I'll teach him a lesson to prove that he's nobody around here. Who does he think he is?" Dudu said. He made sure that no fighter completed all his training with flying colors.

"I want us meet tomorrow morning at 7:00 a.m. and see who the best sharpshooter is," Dudu said through clenched teeth. Dekie was afraid and told Mosquito that he was not going to participate. "He's my commander, and it's a gross insubordination for me to challenge him."

"Go for it, boy, and prove yourself to him," Mosquito urged him. He also would need courage to challenge Dekie after training him.

That night, Dudu thought about Dekie and how he could be of use to their leader. *He's young and brilliant. If the president learns about him, he will hit the top soon. I'll make sure I keep him down as long as I'm the third in command around here. Supposing that kid disgraces me tomorrow? It's impossible! No one, including our field commander, can beat me in a shootout. I proved it in Libya. This rat who can't even hold a gun properly cannot stand before me!*

In the morning, all the trainees and commanders gathered on the field to watch this spectacular event. A brand new thirty-eight-round pistol was handed to Dekie by Dudu.

"It's yours if you pass the second round!" Dudu said and walked away without their eyes meeting. There was a tennis ball in one of the commander's hands. He placed it on a small stick 150 ft away. At the count of five, the general shot without even aiming. The bullet pierced the ball. Dudu smiled slackly.

"I want you to beat him to it, soldier!" Mosquito shouted to Dekie. Dekie closed one eye, took aim, and waited for the countdown. He pressed the trigger and hit the tennis ball. He eased down as he saw the approval on the faces of his onlookers. The second round was a bit difficult for Dekie, but he gained confidence from Mosquito. Another fighter stepped up and threw an orange into the air. Again, Dudu shot without taking aim.

Dekie shook, and his hands were sweaty. A fighter threw another orange in the air. By then, Dekie's focus was up and he was ready. With one eye closed, he took aim again, and the shot shredded the orange in midair. There was approval again but no applause for fear of a backlash from their commander.

The final test was with a live sparrow. The bird was to be released in the air and shot before it got out of sight. Dudu was excellent in this one, but he was overconfident. The bird was released into the air, and it was up where you had to shoot in thirty seconds. Dudu had done this on many occasions. He had beaten his training commander in Libya and won $5,000, but his calculation was wrong this time as he shot without taking aim. He shot and closed his eyes for some seconds before it hit him that he had missed. He missed the living creature by inches, and a few feathers fluttered down. As a professional in the business, he waited for Dekie to miss for another round. The bird happily flew away with joy.

It was now Dekie's turn. There was so much pressure on him. He was afraid to continue, but Mosquito had taught him how to shoot live birds. *Do not take your eyes off the bird. Watch its movements before pulling the trigger,* Dekie thought. A stranger walked up and said, "I'll make you a lieutenant if you can bring down the bird!" It was the rebel field commander. Everyone was surprised to see him.

The field commander, Gen. Yealue, had been watching in amusement without anyone knowing that he was around. His presence brought more pressure on Dekie. But he knew this was his opportunity to climb the ranks. The general took the bird and threw it up. Dekie didn't know where the confidence came from this time, but he didn't aim as he had done before. He shot, and the bird scattered in the air.

A bright smile crossed Mosquito's face. The field commander honored Dekie right there as a lieutenant. "From today, you're Lieutenant Dekie! I've heard a lot about you but today, you've proved yourself. We need you to lead our men!" Gen. Yealue said. He patted Dekie on his shoulder and walked away. Dekie was glad to end the ordeal with his commander. Anxiety and emotion welled up in him as he stood and watched the bird explode into pieces. All of his comrades came around to congratulate him. A voice broke up the celebration. "Lieutenant Dekie, congratulations. Be a man!"

He walked away with a hiss, bowing his head in shame. Dudu had never lost to anyone in his life. In Libya, he had won all the military contests. He was feared by his comrades and students. He never joked or laughed. He felt humiliated before his trainees.

Col. Mosquito stood, smiling, and slowly walked over to Dekie after Dudu left. "Come here, my boy, I'm so proud of you." He embraced Dekie for a long time before releasing him. That night, he cautioned Dekie to be careful with the general. "You humiliated him. He can kill you at any time. Don't ever cross his path. We'll be leaving tomorrow for Sanniquelle and then to Gbarnga and Kakata. You've been selected as one of the men to lead the troops to Salala, Kakata, and Bong Mines. You're the only high-ranking soldier among your comrades, and I expect you to behave well and earn their respect. Remember, they're now watching you. We'll stop in Sanniquelle so you can also see your mom and sisters. I'll give you some cash, but sooner or later, you'll have enough cash and babes!"

Dekie could not believe what had occurred in less than twenty-four hours. *Am I dreaming, or is this how life goes? I thought that I wasn't going to see my mom again, and here I am going see her tomorrow. I'll soon see my family in Gibi also.* He closed his eyes and thought about Nyenea and his family for a long time. *Will I see you all again? I'll get you all out if you are still in Gibi.* He fell asleep.

He had a dream about Saye. He had met Saye in his house, lying down. "I'm not well, but I'm alive, my friend. I escaped from those thieves," Saye had said. Dekie woke up sweating.

"Oh Saye! I hope we meet again!" Dekie said with tears in his eyes. He loved his friend, but whether his friend would still accept him was another thing. Saye had said that only thieves and thugs participated in rebel movements. Saye was the only boy who refused to join the rebels since they had cleared Sanniquelle in the beginning of 1990.

"I have to talk him out of his stubbornness if he's still alive," Dekie said to himself. Dekie was changing by the day as he got entrenched in the movement. He started smoking marijuana and took lots of local drinks to keep himself numb like everyone else.

CHAPTER 3

• • •

KIAMU FLARED UP AND TOLD his nieces about his displeasure with their father's attitude. "Your father will allow the rebels to take over his farm and his family as hostages."

His nieces sat in dead silence, listening to their uncle. They had heard him grumbling about their father for some time now, and they knew that it was working him up.

"I want you all to pray for the family and your grandparents, who will be arriving next week. Let's hope that your grandparents bring Nyenea along," Kaimu said and dismissed the girls. Neneh tried to encourage them but to no avail.

"Our little brother should come with Grandpa and Grandma," Seanee said with tears in her eyes.

"Let's understand Daddy's point too, girls. He's not refusing to leave Liberia. Our dad has invested more than $100,000 on the farm, and he can't just leave it and come here," Jokata said.

"We know, but he should send our mom and Nyenea over at least." The three sisters sat with tears in their eyes.

Mr. Mleh got the visas for his in-laws and came back to contemplate his ordeal. The situation was weighing him down. The effect could be seen in his eyes. His wife really felt sorry for the position that her husband was now in. Nyenea was aware of the situation, but he chose to remain silent because his father had told him to. The rumors about the rebels' next attack were heard everywhere. The schools in Kakata continued having classes. But for how long?

Polan's parents left for the United States in anger because Mr. Mleh refused to let their grandson travel with them. Ma Leneh wanted her grandson to leave Liberia. The girls and Kiamu had planned with them to bring him.

"We may not see this boy again, Polan, and I have had so many bad feelings about him," Ma Leneh said to her daughter in tears. As they boarded the plane, Polan wondered if her mom was right. She waved her last good-bye in uncertainty. On their way back, Mr. Mleh cleared his throat and asked his wife if he was to blame for their tears at the airport.

"My mom believes that the situation may get out of hand, as Kiamu predicts. It may take more than ten years before we see an end to this crisis," Polan said.

"I've gotten our passports ready, my dear. If things don't improve by the end of June, we'll leave," Mr. Mleh promised.

● ● ●

Ma Yah and Ma Kou spent a lot of time together. They felt the same pain and found solace in each other. Residents of Sanniquelle saw the worst form of killings ever in their city's history. No law governed their territory except jungle justice. The gun spoke for everyone. All sympathizers or collaborators with the government were killed without any investigation. All those from the Mandingo tribe were killed if found in Nimba or tried to escape through the bush to Gbarnga or the Republic of Guinea.

The rebels killed them because of their support to President Samuel Doe. President Doe gave recognition to the Mandingo tribe in the eighties as an official tribe of Liberia. Many Mandingos started getting into mainstream politics with President Doe. Their large support for the one seen as the demon to the rebels made them targets.

Life became very miserable for many common citizens in the rebel-controlled territories too. There was no work for parents and no schools for their children. Ma Yah continued to stay indoors since the departure of her son. For more than a month and a half, she kept mourning, thinking that he was dead. After her husband's death, the horror of her son's disappearance was unbearable.

"How can I live without the two most important men in my life?" she asked every time. Her girls, Lulu and Zowahbah, went out to buy and sell food to keep the family going, but they worried about their mom's health often. She and Ma Kou spent the happy and sad days together. Ma Kou would come after work in the local clinic. She was busier than ever, attending to wounded rebel fighters by the hour. After work, she would sit with her friend and they would comfort each other.

One evening, Lulu and Zowahbah brought news from the streets. They saw many of the town's boys climbing down from a captured military truck that had disappeared a month or two before. These boys' mothers cried for them just like their mom did for Dekie. "Ma, today we saw some of the boys who were kidnapped from our town," the girls said. The mothers tried to hide their emotions, but their smiles betrayed them.

"Did you ask any of them about your brother?" Ma Yah asked.

"No, Ma. They didn't want to talk to us, and Ma, they looked different," Lulu answered. More than two hundred small boys from Sanniquelle were seen patrolling the city with guns too big for them to carry. Many parents were happy to see their sons again.

Ma Kou left for her house to find out from her neighbor's son about Saye. She met her neighbor's son sitting with everyone surrounding him like a king in their living room. The boy was twelve years old.

"Opa, did you see your brother Saye?" Ma Kou asked.

"Don't call me Opa! I am a soldier and not a boy anymore! My name is Private Killer!" Little Opa said with disdain on his face. Everyone was shocked to hear the kid speak like that to a woman who was older than his own mother.

"Shut up!" His mother shouted back. Opa got up and walked away without looking back. The overcrowded living room was quiet. Mouths were opened wide in disbelief. Every parent thought that their children were getting some good training from the rebels, and they still saw them as the babies who had been taken few weeks ago, but they had changed into little demons. Opa was high on marijuana mixed with cocaine. They had been taught how to kill without fear or remorse. Ma Kou stood up and asked Opa's mom to please excuse her; she had to go home.

"I'm sorry, Ma Kou," Opa's mom tried to say, but it was too late. Such disrespect brought shame and disgrace to Opa's mom and her friend. Ma Kou reached home and met a stranger.

"Hello. How may I help you?" she asked.

"My name is Quianue from Tepo. I'd prefer that we go inside before I talk, please."

As they entered, Ma Kou was filled with mixed emotions. *Is my son dead?* "Sit down, please. May I bring you some water?"

"Yes, please," Quianue said to reduce the tension.

Ma Kou gave him water and sat, waiting for the news. The town was crowded with all kinds of men and women carrying guns, but there was something different about her visitor.

Mr. Quianue cleared his throat. "Your son Saye sent me to see you."

"My son!" Ma Kou almost jumped out of her seat but kept her cool in case any bad news followed.

"I am a hunter. I found your son a month and a half ago deep in the forest one night," Mr. Quianue narrated the whole story.

"Is he well?" Ma Kou asked.

"Yes, but he's afraid to come out and be killed by the rebels."

Ma Kou was stunned to hear about her son. Saye had always said that he would not be a rebel, destroying other people's lives. "I was going to leave tonight, but if you wish to come and see him, we can go tomorrow," Mr. Quianue said.

"Yes, we can leave tomorrow morning. I'll fix the guest room for you if you don't mind," Ma Kou said and thanked her guest for coming.

"Oh, thanks, but I'll spend the night with my cousin," replied Mr. Quianue. They discussed their trip for the next day and with that, Mr. Quianue said good-bye and left. He warned her not tell anybody because no one was to be trusted anymore.

• • •

Lt. Dekie and Col. Mosquito went on an assignment for Gen. Dudu. Dudu had sent Dekie to test his loyalty. They reached a small village and asked for a Liberian Ivorian trader called Sekou. On his return from the market across the border with Ivory Coast, Sekou met them waiting for him. Sekou was believed to be rich. He traded coffee and cocoa. Living along the border, which belongs to both countries, Sekou, like many of the people living there, claimed dual citizenship. They'd seen themselves as one people until the colonial masters divided them into two countries. Gio and Mano could be heard on both sides of the border. Mosquito took the man inside and came out with a large bundle of cash in US dollars. Sekou was not happy to be robbed. "I'll tell your commander, General Dudu, tomorrow," Sekou threatened.

Mosquito asked Dekie to kill Sekou in his house. Taking orders, Dekie entered the house and told Sekou to lie down on the floor. He shot Sekou in the back of his head and ran out in a rage. He trembled after the incident.

"Calm down, soldier! You don't have to be too hard on yourself. Sooner or later, you'll find pleasure in wasting people!" Mosquito said. Dekie respected his trainer and friend, so he found it hard to disobey his orders. On their way back to the base, he gave Dekie $1,000 from the loot. "We have some food prepared for us at home. You should feel free and enjoy yourself, Lieutenant! You're good to go now!" Mosquito said as he passed the marijuana over to Dekie to cool off. "We'll be leaving tomorrow instead of today. Dudu has promised that we'll leave at all cost."

At the house, the food was ready and set before them. Dekie was so high on the drug that he ate without looking into the bowl. He enjoyed eating the food with lots of meat. Mosquito watched him with pleasure as his boy ate the flesh and heart of the little girl from the village. After that, Dekie slept for most of the day, high on the mixed weed and cocaine. This was a test for one who had come high in their ranks. To be a good member of their demonic rebel movement, you had to prove your resilience and courage to your commander as a true warrior by eating the flesh of a human being and killing others with pleasure. The NPFL rebels became the most ruthless modern-day cannibals. They used drugs as a tool to keep the young fighters' brains dead to reality. Depraved people and rejects in the society quickly embraced such an evil organization.

The next morning by six o'clock, the trucks were ready to leave for Sanniquelle. Dudu warned Dekie to be careful with the lives of the men who would soon be entrusted to him, "You should work with Mosquito and respect him as your superior officer."

Dekie thought of all the wonderful things that he had wanted to achieve in life such as education and a family to call his own. Now, here he sat with $1,000 in his pocket for killing someone. He had never seen or owned that kind of cash in his life. A sad thought of who he had become flooded his mind. Just as his friend Saye said, "Only thieves and thugs belong to such a movement." He had become as ruthless as the other rebels.

Ma Kou considered whether she should share her good news with her friend, Ma Yah. That evening before she left, she finally said to her friend, "I'll be traveling tomorrow morning to a village called Tepo."

"Oh, I know Tepo Village. What are you going to do there?" Ma Yah asked. Since her friend Ma Kou came back from visiting her neighbor's house, she had noticed some excitement in her friend's voice. This was the question that Ma Kou dreaded from her friend. She spilled it out flatly. "I'm going to see Saye."

She quickly explained everything to avoid further questions. Ma Yah was shocked as she listened. Unable to speak, she burst into tears. Both of them started crying as Zowahbah and Lulu entered. Of course, it was nothing new or strange to see them crying, but not in the evening. Ma Kou returned home late that night.

Early the next day, Quianue was at her door. They left by six for the four-hour journey.

"You have a very brave son. We need many young people like that," Quianue said. He told her that his son he too had been taken away almost two months before. The journey was long for Ma Kou, but she found it interesting and was confident in talking to this stranger. Ma Yah had earlier warned her to be careful because no one was trusted in Liberia.

"Not this man," Ma Kou had told her friend. "There's something genuine about him." But she knew that her friend was concerned about her well-being.

A Nissan pickup truck was parked in front of Ma Yah's house when Lulu poked her head out to see who it was. She quickly pushed the door open and ran out to greet her brother, Dekie. He embraced her for a long time before releasing her. He was happy to see her again too.

"We missed you, brother, and Mama has been crying since you and Saye left. Where's Saye?" she asked and instantly saw the sad look that quickly appeared on his face. No one said a word until they entered the house.

Ma Yah jumped to her feet to greet her son. This was the first time that the girls saw their mother being happy since the pitiful night of his disappearance. "Thank God that you're alive, Dekie. I'm so glad to see you," his mom said with a broad smile on her face. Zowahbah came in from the road after hearing about her brother's return from a neighbor. "Oh brother! Thank God we can see you again," she said.

Dekie went out and returned with Mosquito. "Ma, this is my commander, Col. Zokaya. He has been a good friend to me, and he's a wonderful person."

Col. Mosquito refused to make himself known as Mosquito to Dekie's mom. He was courteous to Dekie's mother. "You have a wonderful son, Ma, and he's one of our best soldiers." He sat for a while and left. Dekie escorted him to the car and came back up to tell his mother about Saye's death.

"Ma, my friend Saye didn't make it. He got killed when he tried to escape from our kidnappers the night they took us. I have to go and see his mom right now."

His mother was silent for a time before telling her son to settle down. "Saye is alive, my son. His mother left this morning to see him at Tepo Village."

"What? Oh, I can't believe this! My friend is alive! I want to see my friend Saye before I leave," Dekie said. He was so happy.

He tried to explain to his mom that he had decided to stay with NPFL until the end.

"Are you sure, my son? This is going to get worse. You could get your-self killed. This is a dangerous movement that has already taken many lives, and you want to make me a woman without a son for the rest of my life."

He knew that his mother would oppose his decision. She hated vio-lence. She had always told him to stay away from the dangerous student groups on BWI campus. He found it difficult to convince his mom at that moment or to tell her about his rise in the NPFL in such a short time. He decided that wouldn't make any difference, so he kept his mouth shut about his achievement. "Ma, the government's soldiers are killing our peo-ple every day. More than two hundred of our fellow Gios and Manos were massacred in the Lutheran church in Sinkor, Monrovia, with many more beheaded every day in and around the city. I have to help our people, Ma."

"Can you save our people?" his mother asked in a harsh tone. He knew where his mother was heading. She never had money to give him, but she always spoke her mind. "If you're asking me, I want you to leave them and run off with us to Ivory Coast. Ma Kou and I are planning to move there by the end of this month."

Dekie was not ready to abandon what he saw as fun within the space of a month and a half. At the age of nineteen, he was leading a troop, and they all respected him enough to do anything he commanded. "OK, Ma. You can take my sisters, and I'll follow after I reach my family in Gibi," he lied to escape his mother's hard truths, which had not changed since he was a child.

His mother changed the topic because it was not going too well for either of them. "I can send someone with you to see Saye if you want."

"Thanks, Mom. Please don't be angry with me over my decision," Dekie said. They talked about other things and planned the trip for his mother to Ivory Coast. He gave her the $1,000 from Mosquito and promised to get more cash for her later to use in Ivory Coast until he joined them.

"Where did you get such an amount from, Dekie?" she asked. He lied to his mother about the money. His mother took the money and sent for one of her neighbors to ask about Tepo. Her neighbor was in his fifties but still looked strong.

"I'll take him tomorrow morning," Dhan said.

Ma Kou and Quianue reached Tepo late in the afternoon. Her son was sleeping. As soon as she put down her bag containing his clothes and medicine, she burst into tears. Ma Norn took her away and tried to calm her down. She was very thankful to them for saving the life of her only child. When they were still on their way, she thought at one point that she was going to see someone else instead of her son. Saye woke up to see his mother seated by him with tears in her eyes.

"Oh my Saye! I'm so glad to see you," Ma Kou said. Saye started crying too.

She brought some pain-killers and other tablets for his infection. She took a look at his wounds and applied some liquid antibiotics to clean them up. She knew that he needed to be taken to a hospital for an X-ray in case there were bullets in his body or a broken bone. She wasn't too sure if the bullets were close to his kidney.

"You may have a damaged kidney," she said with tears in her eyes. Saye thought of that dreadful night when he ran from their house. He thought he would never see his mom again. "I'm alive, Ma. God used this family to save my life and keep me alive till today."

It was an emotional reunion that kept Ma Norn and her husband watching from a distance. Their effort had not been in vain. Ma Norn cried too as she watched. Ma Kou wiped her tears and sat quietly, staring at her son as if they had just met for the first time after many years. He and his mom spent many hours talking and trying to catch up.

Saye knew that his mother was worried, because it was written all over her face. She had lost weight since he'd last seen her. He quickly thought of Dekie. "Mom, they took Dekie away that night. After I escaped, I felt ashamed of not escaping with him, and I've been blaming myself since that day. I feel that I betrayed him. I hope to see him one day and make amends for what happened that night," Saye said.

"Dekie's mother and I have been spending our time together since you two left. I leave my house by dawn for work and return by 5:00 p.m. to her house. I stay there until it is late. We share whatever little we have to eat," his mother explained. He felt sorry for her because she had been the breadwinner of the family since the death of his father.

"When you left that night, the freedom fighters took over the city and canceled the curfew. There was jubilation on the streets of Sanniquelle. Many people, including Mr. Sirleaf and his family from the Mandingo tribe, were killed," his mom said. Mr. Sirleaf was a family friend.

The next morning, she planned to return to Sanniquelle and work out a way of getting her son to Ivory Coast for treatment. His wounds were healing too slowly, and he probably had an infection. Saye and his mother were seated on his mattress when Ma Norn came in and announced that they had a visitor. Saye didn't know anyone in the village, and his mother was a stranger too. Who could their visitor be?

Dekie came alone without a bodyguard or a gun to see his friend. Mosquito had objected to his trip but gave in. He and his escort, Dhan, had left Sanniquelle by four o'clock in the morning. Since his arrival in Sanniquelle the day before, he had not used any drug. He looked sober but had an unkempt beard and bushy hair.

"Good morning," Dekie said, smiling at his friend. Saye thought he was dreaming again. He closed his eyes and opened them again to make sure that it was his friend. They hugged for a long time. There were tears in their eyes as they stood, looking at each other. They had always loved each other. The revolution was the first stumbling block of their friendship. On his way to see Saye, Dekie had decided to respect his friend's view about the war, no matter what it was, and help him get to a hospital.

He noticed that his friend's body had grown very lean. "I'm sorry, man, about the incident that night. I thought I could have done something, but I was against an army like a toothless bulldog after an armed robber," Dekie said with tears in his eyes. Saye replied, "Yeah, I'm sorry too for leaving you alone that night. I felt a sense of betrayal. Please, forgive me for my actions." Dekie always felt complete around his friend.

Worried about Saye's condition, Dekie thought about what he could do. He cried for a long time and turned to Ma Kou. "My mom told me about what you two have been going through. Let's plan a way out for my friend now before it's too late. We've got to get him to a hospital as soon as possible. I'm willing to do anything to get him out." He had not said anything about his training. He decided to leave that out.

• • •

Mr. and Mrs. Sumo arrived in the United States and were greeted by their son and grandchildren. Everyone had expected to see little Nyenea, but to their dismay, he was not on board. Mr. Fhan Sumo expressed his feelings before everyone. "If anything happens to Nyenea, I'll hold his father responsible." He was angry about Mr. Mleh's refusal to let Nyenea travel with them. Nyenea's sisters were sad, but they could do nothing about the situation from the United States.

"Let's pray for them, everybody. We can't do anything else," Kiamu said. Kiamu's parents described the situation and its effect on the people. They hoped to talk to the Mleh family one last time before the rebels overran their farm.

• • •

Yeanue was assigned to Gbarnga City, the capital city of Bong County, after its capture. He thought of how to get a message to his parents. It had been almost three months since he'd last seen them. He knew that his father was against him going for training, and he wouldn't have allowed it if he had not been out hunting that night. He had been taken away as his mother cried out for him.

He had watched the murder of two other friends before they reached their destination in Botuwou. He had not fully given himself over to the movement. He knew the facts about the rebels' activities and how destructive they were. Yeanue saw himself as an alien wandering in the wrong territory. He disagreed with all their rules and had it at the back of his mind that he was in the wrong place at the wrong time. He dreamed every night about his death. He refused to take orders from his superior officers every time he was asked to kill someone.

He was sent out on an operation one night with two other boys. They raided a Lebanese businessman's house and stole more than $50,000. He was then asked to kill the man and his family. He entered the house and shot his Beretta at the ceiling. He came out, running for his comrades to follow.

In fact, when he had entered the house, he asked the man and his family to go to a nearby house and promised that he would get them out of Gbarnga the next day. He kept his promise, but a week later, his ruse was discovered, and he was imprisoned indefinitely. He decided that it was time to jump out of the force, and nothing was going to stop him. *I've seen enough destruction in the space of two months. I need to get out!* Yeanue thought.

When he met Mr. Quianue and his wife, Dekie just stood there, staring at them. He saw the strong resemblance between Yeanue and Quianue. It was a strange stare that left everyone thinking.

"Is something wrong, Dekie?" Saye asked.

"No, I met a boy on the base called Yeanue."

Ma Norn didn't wait for him to finish his statement. "Yes! He's our son. He looks just like his father! Where's he now?" she asked with a big grin on her face. There was a big celebration in the little mud house that had been sad since the departure of their son. Saye and the family had planned to leave for Ivory Coast before the arrival of his mother and his friend. The celebration ended with tears in Dekie's eyes. He tried desperately to hide them but his friend knew that there was something eating him up.

Everyone Dekie knew and loved hated the war and spoke against its evil. Even Yeanue didn't think that it was a justified war. Yeanue once told him that the rebel leader's children were not on the base with them. He had thought about that statement for a long time after Yeanue left for Gbarnga.

"I'll contact your son Yeanue as soon as I get to Gbarnga," Dekie promised Mr. Quianue and his wife. "We became friends on the base, so I think we're all one big family now." Ma Norn was the happiest mother in the house. She thanked God, bowing down on the dirt floor with her hands up. The mothers held hands, tears rolling down from their eyes.

Dekie felt good for putting a smile on the faces of these proud mothers.

A plan was drawn up for their four hours trip back to Sanniquelle. Saye had to be carried by Dekie on his back like a baby. It was a terrible trip that was done by night. Before leaving that evening, Quianue informed some friends in the village about a quick trip to Sanniquelle and said he would be back in a week. He had to lie because the village had many loyalists to the rebel movement. Some saw him as a traitor after he expressed his dissatisfaction over the abduction of his son. The trip was slow because of Saye and the women.

They reached Sanniquelle by midnight. The city was very quiet. In Dekie's mother's house, they were greeted with joy as everyone gathered to see Saye. The house should have been quiet in order to avoid attention, but it was too late. A knock was heard on the front door in less than five minutes after their arrival.

"Open this door, or I'll bring it down!" a voice shouted. Dekie didn't want his family and his friend to know what he had become, so he quietly asked everyone to wait in the living room while he dealt with the situation. He opened the door without speaking to the men and stepped outside.

"It is fine here, soldiers. I'm here with my family, and everything is OK!" Lt. Dekie said through clenched teeth.

"Who are you?" the leader asked.

"I'm Lieutenant Dekie Woodor, assigned to Colonel Mosquito!"

It took a while before the group's leader could speak. Lt. Dekie was well known by many of his compatriots, and his name had spread throughout the rebel territory like wildfire after the defeat of Gen. Dudu. He was the only recruit to have such a high rank. The leader of the group and his men saluted him.

"At ease, soldiers!" Lt. Dekie released them and opened the door. Saye was standing behind him, shocked. He could not find the right words to address his friend.

"Look, I know what you're thinking, but maybe my participation in this war is to bring good to you and my family for now." Dekie spoke without looking at his friend. Saye instantly felt sorry for his friend and decided to leave him with his convictions, but he didn't agree with him. Saye hugged his friend and led him to the living room. As they held hands, Dekie felt like going with them to the Ivory Coast and forgetting about the senseless war.

"I'll join you all soon, but first let me go to Gibi and get my family from there." Dekie lied to them just as he had lied to his mom.

He knew that it was now impossible for him to turn back as he now saw life differently from his friend. The long-term education that his parents could not afford had been forgotten in such a short time. Mosquito had promised to give him $10,000 if he went with him on a mission the next day. The $1,000 that he had earlier given his mom was not enough for all of them. From that operation, he planned to get his friend and family to Ivory Coast. They slept together in the living room that night, talking until sleep overtook them by three.

At six o'clock, Mosquito came for Dekie. They went out on the mission and returned by noon. Everything went as planned. A boy led them to a Mandingo trader hiding in one village. He had lots of property and businesses in Nimba. He had a gas station in Saniquille and Ganta and Tapeta. The boy had been one of his workers in his gas station in Sanniquelle. Dekie killed the man and his family in cold blood.

Mosquito stood there, smiling as his lieutenant butchered the family. "Good job, boy!" Dekie's clothes were bloody after the assault. "I'll take you to my house to clean up and change."

At Mosquito's house, the money was counted, and $10,000 was given to Dekie. He smiled as he took the money from his commander. "Thank you, sir." He spent more time in his commander's house so that the drugs he took for the trip could wear off from his brain.

● ● ●

Mr. Mleh and his family were now edgy. There were daily rumors of the rebels taking over Salala. Salala is the largest town before Gibi. If Salala was taken, they would be next in line for capture by the rebels. They had heard about the atrocities committed by the rebels. Mr. Mleh had promised his wife to leave at the end of May, but it was not getting better. There was fear throughout the countryside as the rebels advanced. Mr. Mleh thought about his son's future if the rebels took over their farm.

Am I being too selfish? Am I afraid to face reality? The situations strained their relationship. Polan kept thinking about their son and how he might not understand what was going on. She wanted Nyenea to leave with her parents, but she had already accepted her husband's decision. She didn't agree with him, but she gave up. "Our son's life may end up under the terror of the rebels," Polan said. She had been worried since the news about the rebels taking Gbarnga came because their farm was located along the way to Kakata. She and her husband had stopped arguing about the war and their trip to the United States when she could not convince him.

That evening Dekie came home with a bag of US parboiled rice and some fresh meat and fish for the family. Everyone stayed at Ma Yah's house. Mr. Quianue and his wife, Ma Norn, and Ma Kou and her son, Saye, spent the day at the house. Zowahbah and Lulu cooked while the others sat in the living room, planning their trip. Dekie was leaving the next day for Gbarnga, so they all had to leave on the same day.

There was a small quiet party that night.

Dekie arranged for some of his boys to take them to the border town of Logatou early in the morning. Saye and his friend did a lot of talking.

"You're not a freedom fighter. As soon as you get to your family in Gibi, get out of this mess!" Saye advised.

Dekie gave $2,000 to Saye for his medication and $1,500 to Saye's mom. He gave $1,500 to Quianue and his wife and an additional $5,000 to his own mom. "I want you all to live together as one family until I come." Everything was arranged for them to leave the next day. As early as five o'clock the next morning, the looted Toyota pickup truck came for them. Dekie escorted them out of town. Ma Yah called her son aside and warned him. "Dekie, please join us later. I'm already missing you." She hugged her son and felt weak for some reason. Dekie hugged Saye and said good-bye to all.

Back at his commander's house, Lt. Dekie was relieved that they had left.

"Are they gone?" Col. Mosquito asked.

"Yes, sir, and thanks for everything," Dekie said.

Mosquito never saw himself as doing much for Dekie, but Dekie was doing a lot for him. All the dirty jobs were now done by Dekie as he sat on the fence and watched. He only collected or received the cash and gave a little of that to Dekie. "Get all your men ready now. We'll be leaving in an hour," Mosquito commanded.

There was no problem along the road for Dekie's family and friends. There were many people walking on the road to Logatou due to the lack of transportation. All the cars moving within the rebels' territory were owned by them and not by civilians. By noon, they had crossed the border into Nyegleh in Ivory Coast. They took a taxi to Danane, the first big town. The town was getting crowded with many Liberians, mainly from Nimba County. The town was bigger and more beautiful than Sanniquelle. There was electricity, piped-in water, and transportation in the town—something that was not the case in Sanniquelle. The driver took them to the UNHCR head office and left them there.

Lt. Dekie, his commander, and their men arrived in Gbarnga in the afternoon. There were plans to work on. Col. Mosquito and Lt. Dekie reported to the commander in the city and got to work. They began to put a strategy together for an attack on Salala, Bong Mines, and Kakata. As the commanders discussed their next move, Lt. Dekie went out to find Yeanue. Yeanue had been imprisoned right in the same yard where the meeting was held.

As he walked out and asked for Yeanue, he met one of Yeanue's comrades. "Hey, where's Yeanue?"

"Eh...sir, he's in prison," the boy replied. The boy knew Lt. Dekie but since they were not in uniform, it was difficult to know who was who. He gave a description of the cell and left at once. Dekie found the cell where Yeanue was kept. Dekie was now in a different environment where he was not easily recognized as a lieutenant. So, he removed the badge from his pocket and taped it to his cap. The first two rebels who passed saluted him.

At the cell, he was saluted and ushered in by a corporal. "I am here to see Yeanue," Lt. Dekie said. Yeanue was brought out with his hands tied behind his back (*tabay*, as it was called). After their brief discussion, Lt. Dekie promised to get him out by evening. He noticed the sad look on his face and thought, *I'll give him some money to go to Ivory Coast and join his family. This indeed is not his war.* Yeanue had spent ten days in the cell. He was brought out and handed over to Col. Mosquito.

"Thanks again, Colonel, for helping me out," Lt. Dekie said.

"No problem, Lieutenant," Col. Mosquito said and returned to continue his business.

Dekie and Yeanue went to sit aside and talk. "Yeanue, your family saved my friend's life. We're now brothers. Your parents left for Ivory Coast along with my family and my friend today. I want you to go and join your parents."

Yeanue could not believe what he just heard. With a broad smile, he thanked his senior officer and friend. "How are my parents? I really miss them."

"They're doing well, but they need you more than NPFL, and you also need to go back to school."

"I've been planning to run away. I know it's dangerous, but I was going to make an attempt. I'm very glad that God is using you to answer my prayers. I'll never ever forget you. Thank you again," Yeanue said with tears of joy.

Mosquito and Dekie drafted a fake letter to Gen. Dudu for Yeanue to use as an escape ticket to Ivory Coast. Yeanue was to show the letter at any checkpoint for free passage. He was placed on a pickup truck headed for Sanniquelle. Yeanue wore his blue jeans and red T-shirt. Underneath his red T-shirt, he had another T-shirt on and short pants under his blue jeans. On their way to Sanniquelle, they got to a checkpoint with a pregnant woman standing in the midst of some rebels. Some of the rebels were fighting among themselves about whether the woman was carrying a boy or a girl. To solve the problem, the most senior rebel in the pickup truck decided to open up the woman's belly to see the sex of the child.

Cpl. Dollo slashed the woman's belly open as soon as her clothes were removed. He pulled out her intestines and opened up her womb.

"It's a boy!" Dollo announced. Yeanue's stomach clenched, and he felt a sharp pain in his chest. He ran to vomit near the road in order not to be seen by his comrades. This was his first time he had ever seen anything like this. The rest of the rebels standing by shouted a warlike song and danced over winning the bet. Before their pickup truck took off, Dollo shot the woman's husband in the head. The husband had his hands tied behind his back and had been forced to watch his wife being killed. The boys sang and danced around Yeanue as the car sped off. Yeanue was sick for the rest of the trip, but he fought hard not to show his uneasiness. He remained silent and paranoid until they got to Sanniquelle.

His next ride was even harder than the first ride. He had to get into a car going to Logatou and not to Butowou where Gen. Dudu was based. If he got into a car heading in a direction other than what was stated in his letter, he would have been to be apprehended for a different intention. He went and bought another envelope and changed the address to the commander of Logatou.

He saw an old pickup truck loading for Logatou. "Hello. My name is Private Yeanue. May I see the commander for this car?"

"I am the CO," said a very hard-looking face with set jaws.

"I have a letter from Colonel Zokaya to deliver to the commander of Logatou. May I have a ride with you, sir?" Yeanue lied.

"Sure, my name is Dead Body Bone," the corporal said.

Yeanue's ride to Logatou was even worse than the first. He saw the beheading of hundreds of people accused of being members of the Mandingo ethnic group. At every checkpoint, the rebels asked the civilians for their names and tribes. If they mentioned a tribe or a name that the rebels were not satisfied with, the people were put aside and killed immediately.

On getting to the border, he quickly got off and was lost in the crowd. Civilians leaving the country were allowed to cross over the border freely. He entered a bathroom as a rebel and came out as a civilian. He hid his gun in his jeans and the red T-shirt behind the toilet. He crossed the border. As he boarded a bus heading to Danane, he heard from some new arrivals from the border that a gun had been found wrapped with a pair of blue jeans and a T-shirt in a bathroom. They were searching for the freedom fighter who had brought a letter for the commander.

The bus moved away with Yeanue finally breathing a sigh of relief. "Thank God for Mosquito and Dekie that I am now free at last." He even thought of Martin Luther King Jr.'s quote:

"Free at last, free at last, Thank God Almighty,
I'm free at last."

● ● ●

Mosquito and Dekie led their troops to Salala and overran the town.

With the GMG fifty-caliber machine gun, Dekie had stormed the gate with heavy firepower, backed by a few of his men. He had bulldozed his way through the gate and headed straight for the town. The small barracks on the outskirts of town surrendered with the few soldiers who were seen on their arrival. They tried to resist, but many fled with the news of his superior firepower. When Salala was fully under rebel control,

Dekie mapped out the town for any remaining government soldiers. He reported to Mosquito, who waited for them on the highway before getting to the town.

Satisfied by the performance of his boy, he gave Dekie the thumbs up. After that, they headed to Bong Mines through the bush. Dekie had wanted to lead the troop to Gibi to rescue his family, but it was not a strategic place, so he had to go with his commander to Bong Mines. They passed through the Bong Mountain range and entered the town.

"That was a brilliant move, boy, but you have a tougher job ahead in Bong Mines," Mosquito said with a grim smile on his face.

Dekie crossed the town through the bush and led his troops from the entry point to Bong Mine's police checkpoint. They took over the checkpoint and wore the police uniforms. Later, they ambushed a military truck from Kakata and changed their police uniforms to AFL military camouflage. He led his troops in the military truck to the J. D. K. Baker Junior High School at the entrance of Bong Mines and set up a checkpoint there. He asked one of his best fighters called Dave to join him and the driver. As their truck arrived at the BMC security gate which was now occupied by government military personnel, he asked Dave to back him up. He told Dave to remain in the truck. As soon as he got down, there were fifteen government soldiers coming to attack. He single-handedly took down all fifteen soldiers with his pistol.

Dave could not believe what he had just witnessed. He had never seen his leader in serious action before. He thought that he was watching a war movie. His leader fought and dodged bullets at the same time. His victims fell, bullets in their foreheads. The driver stood there with his mouth wide open as he watched their leader bring down armed soldiers like robots.

"He cleared the checkpoint in a flash," Dave said to the driver. Dekie advanced toward the security booth and pointed his reloaded pistol at five soldiers huddled together. They held up their hands in surrender. "We beg you, sir. Please, spare our lives." He remembered what his commander had said: "Don't keep any of Doe's soldiers alive!"

He asked the them to come out with their hands up and get into the truck. As soon as he came back to the truck, Dekie said, "Dave, don't let anybody know about these soldiers! Hey, where are you all from?"

"We are all volunteer soldiers from here in Bong Mines," they said.

"Go home to your parents at once!" Lt. Dekie felt so sorry for the young faces that he had almost killed. *They ran away from me because they are all volunteer soldiers and not trained soldiers for President Doe.* Again his heart ached when he saw their youth being wasted by leaders who did not care about them.

Mosquito and his troops never met any resistance from the workstation to Zaweita and then in Botota. He sent some rebels on reconnaissance to Bong Town and Nyehn. They met with Dekie at the hospital. They exchanged information and reported back to their base. Mosquito and his deputy, Dekie, met at the swimming pool that evening to talk.

"Great job, boy, I'm really proud of you," Col. Mosquito said. "I've told the president about you already, but he has an assignment for you. There's a problem going on now. There's been a breakup within the NPFL. The president does not want you to leave the NPFL movement for another. The field commander who gave you the rank of lieutenant has resigned from NPFL and is on his way to Monrovia."

Dekie sat there silently watching his commander. "What does the president want me to do?"

"The president wants to set up a marine training base at German Camp in Gibi. I thought you wanted to go there. If so, you're going there as their commander," Mosquito said firmly.

Dekie thought at first that he did not hear his commander right. "Sir, how can I command a base when there are better trained fighters than I?" Dekie asked his commander and friend.

Mosquito thought about the fears of his junior officer for a long time before saying, "We have a dinner to attend at the horse club tonight with the manager of Bong Mining Company."

At the party, Dekie sat for a long time and stared around. He had never been to such a party before. There were more white people than blacks at the party. The food was great. They were given some cash as a present, and a house was selected for them. For the first time in his life, Dekie slept in an air-condition house.

That night, Dekie tried to go over the events of the day. His first real fight had been done with ease. He felt as if there was a force controlling him. He had no fear of his enemies, and all his shots were on target. He thought about what his commander had said about the new base. *It's a good idea. I'll get my family out of Gibi.*

CHAPTER 4

• • •

SAYE WAS HOSPITALIZED BY THE time they got a house on the second day in Danane. There was still a bullet in his back. The infection from his wounds had destroyed his one of his kidneys. The United Nations High Commission for Refugees (UNHCR) took Saye to Abidjan, the Ivorian capital, for treatment. Upon their arrival, he was admitted but warned that he had less than two weeks to live. He needed a kidney transplant, which could not be performed in Abidjan.

"It's a miracle that he's still alive. He could have died from the damaged kidney and infection," the doctor said. Saye's mom waited outside for the result. "Mom, your son has to be taken abroad for further treatment, or he'll die."

Mom Kou sat with tears in her eyes. "What can I do? His father is dead, and I don't have the money to send him."

"The UNHCR will sponsor his trip to the United States and his medical bills, but first you have to give us the full story of what happened to him," the UNHCR representative said.

She gave a full description of what happened from the day that strange men kept coming to get her son to his escape from them and their trip to Ivory Coast.

"When we got to the house in Danane, he fell asleep and didn't wake up again until we got to the UNHCR office to ask for help," Mom Kou explained. Saye was taken to the United States the next week by the UNHCR. His mom returned to the rest of the family in Danane and met

Yeanue, the son of Quianue and Ma Norn. She shared the good news with them and joined in the celebration of Yeanue's return.

● ● ●

Mosquito and Dekie went to Gibi to set up the base. The plan was to use the German rubber plantation staff housing as a permanent training base and to train the meanest and toughest fighters to fear nothing. Dekie was seen as the one who never feared a gun or a soul alive. Their trip went through Kakata and Gibi. Mosquito and Dekie passed through BWI school campus to see their beloved school deserted after being captured a week ago. They drove around for a while and headed to Gibi.

"The president will be in Bong Mines tomorrow. On his way back to Gbarnga, he'll stop by to see us. You have to do everything possible and promise your complete loyalty to him. He's going to give you a promotion, based upon my recommendation. I have already told him that you single-handedly captured Salala and Bong Mines. He has lots of confidence in you, so don't screw it up now! I know you can make it anywhere. The skills and tactics in you are God-given talents," Mosquito said.

Dekie stood there, thinking about the evil that he felt growing inside him. Now this evil was being referred to as God-given. *I'm becoming a demon day by day, drinking human blood and eat human organs and flesh almost on a daily basis.* Yet he found himself giving in to its enticement. He had had his first meal with people that he could never say hi to or even stand within a hundred yards of them. He started to see himself as an important figure now in the movement, with the rebel leader wanting to meet him.

They arrived in Gibi and were met by Lt. Killer.

He was waiting for their arrival. "How was your trip, sir?" Lt. Killer asked.

"You can leave tonight for Kakata, Killer!" Col. Mosquito ordered.

Killer got into a brand-new Nissan pickup truck with his troops and left. Dekie looked at the pickup truck for a long time and finally realized where he knew it from. *It's Mr. Mleh's new truck.* But it was too late as his

71

compatriots were long gone. He instantly started out for the Mlehs' farm to find them. If their car was out here, it meant they were also off the farm.

He knew what he and his comrades were capable of. The first things they often got were cars, money, and electronics. He got permission from his boss and sped off quickly to the Mlehs' farm. When he arrived, he could not believe the level of destruction that had been done to the farm. The house had been destroyed from the roof to the floor. The farm lay in ruins. There were no chickens or pigs. The machines at the factory were gone, and the warehouse had been completely burned to the ground. There was no one to ask. On their way back, he saw one of the daily workers returning to the farm.

As soon as he slowed down, the man started running away from them. Dekie called his former fellow worker by name, "James!"

"Dekie! How are you?" James said as he came closer to them.

"I'm fine, James. Where's the family?" Dekie moved closer to James without his gun.

"They took our boss and his wife away, but Nyenea is at my house right now," James said.

"Take me there now," Dekie said.

They sped off to James's house. Nyenea was sitting all by himself. Dekie could not believe it when he saw his little friend. They hugged for a long time before Nyenea pulled away. "They took my parents away, Dekie!" The boy's cry rang deep in Dekie's ears as he came back to the reality of life once more. Since he'd met the family, they had been so good together that he just could not believe what the war was doing to ordinary families.

I've seen so many families torn apart by this conflict. "Get in the car, Nyenea. We'll find your parents," he said. They left for the compound where the managers used to live. Dekie was given a house just like the one he spent the night in at Bong Mines. There was electricity, piped-in water, a satellite dish, and many cars for him. The company expatriates had been driven out when the plantation was captured two weeks ago.

As they entered the house, Dekie noticed that his little friend was afraid of his bodyguards and their guns. He called his bodyguards and cautioned them about their presence around the boy.

• • •

The two weeks that had passed since the capture of the farm were terrible for Mr. Mleh and Polan. They found it difficult to adapt to their new life. They had not seen their son since they had been picked up and accused of being officials of President Samuel Doe's government. Mr. Mleh had pleaded with his attackers as he tried to prove his innocence. "We're farmers, not government officials. I used to work for the Bong Mining Company."

He was beaten and dragged to another pickup truck. His house was looted of everything of value, including his cars and all the cash they had in the house. Their son was out on the farm when the rebels got to the house. They were taken to Salala and put in a small room with other alleged government officials and later transferred to Gbarnga.

Their crime was not specified to them, but the rebels were arresting all government officials such as the police, immigration officers, and ministry employees, and all relatives of any individuals in government. The young boys used as rebel fighters were not on salary. Therefore, they were told by their commanders to loot in order to get paid. They would charge you just to get all that you had. If your house was a modern type, you were forced out and prevented from ever returning to it. All the fighters wanted the cars. If there was more than one car, the fighter would give one to his commander or take all. The charge against the Mleh family was because of their property and not because they were government officials.

After a week in the cell, Polan developed pneumonia from sleeping on the cold floor. As her health deteriorated, her husband worried because he could not do anything about it.

I should have listened to her and the rest of her family. I'll be blamed if anything happens to her, Mr. Mleh thought. Their accusers had earlier rejected his request to seek medical assistance for his wife, but she was finally admitted to the Phebe Hospital after intervention by another rebel who felt sorry for her. She cried for her children, saying how she might never see them again. Her voice was hoarse and weak, and she found it difficult to breathe and speak at the same time. She fought desperately for her life. "Please find our son and get yourselves out of this terror," Polan said, out of breath. She died a week later from the illness.

Mr. Mleh cried bitterly as he buried his wife with help from a couple of inmates who dug a shallow grave. Life became like an enemy to Mr. Mleh. He was literally going mad when another inmate he had met took him home after they were released. Mr. Kollie Varkpeh felt sorry for him after the death of his wife. Mr. Varkpeh had been a businessman.

"My wife was raped and my three children beheaded before my very eyes on the day Gbarnga was captured. They thought I had money, so they arrested me. We have to see how we can get out of this country now, or we'll be next," Mr. Varkpeh said.

"I can't leave the country without my son," Mr. Mleh said firmly.

His wife's death was a big blow to him. He could not accept the fact that they had been together only two weeks before, and now he had buried her in an unknown place without any representative from her family. He could not face telling her family of their daughter's sad end. He worried about their son and where he could be. He had thought the rebels were only coming for President Doe, but their aim was to destroy the very people that they claimed to liberate. He thought about going to Ivory Coast with his friend in sorrow, Mr. Varkpeh, but he could not leave his son in Gibi.

"How can I leave the country without my son? I have to keep my promise to my dying wife. I'll hang around until I get my boy back." Life had changed in an instant. "I've brought all this on myself. I should have listened to everyone. Now our farm is lying in ruins! My wife is dead, and my son is missing. Oh God, please help me!" He cried through the sleepless nights.

● ● ●

"Nyenea, you have to stay with me until I get your parents and send all of you out of the country," Dekie said.

"I want to stay with you. I'm not going anywhere, Dekie!" Little Nyenea said firmly. Dekie had been trying to get people out of hot spots but he didn't know how to deal with this present situation.

"We have to find your parents, Nyenea, and get you to a safer place than here. My mom and sisters are now in Ivory Coast."

"Why didn't you go with them if it's safer there?" Nyenea asked with a stern look in his eyes.

"I came to get you and your family. I promised to come back for you, right?" Dekie said. He saw that they were going in circles, with the boy getting more defiant. It pained his heart to see that a fifteen-year-old kid could not comprehend the horrors and evil that he had seen in the last three months. The rebel leader's visit to the German camp in Gibi was brief and unlike a normal president's visit. Most of the occupants of the houses owned by the company had been evicted or killed. With all the brutal actions that the rebel leader saw, he didn't bat an eye one bit or frown at his fighters. Instead, he encouraged his men to be more vicious and daring. He promoted Lt. Dekie to colonel and Col. Mosquito to a full general. The program was short and without a speech, but he boosted his men's morale to take the country and rule. The leader himself was high on drugs, just like his followers.

He wore a bulletproof jacket and was flanked by some huge young boys who looked like robots. The rebel leader's complexion looked like that of a mulatto or half-caste. A short man of about five feet tall, he had hair that matched the freckles on his face. He gave out ranks to his gangsters like God filling the skies with stars. To continue killing and getting closer to his objective of being president by hook or crook, he had to please them in every possible way with loot, drugs, sex, and ranks that made them feel as important as official soldiers.

"The country will be ruled by you all very soon! We'll march to Monrovia gallantly and take it by next month!" the rebel leader said. There were chants and whistles from his men as he spoke. To Dekie, the new colonel, he added, "Son, I'm very proud of you. I need more men like you to finish the job. I brought you a little gift of two Land Rover jeeps and this envelope for your courage. You have to promise me to carry out all duties. The aim of this base is to cause harm to anyone who stands in our way. I want to trust you for that. You should lead your men by example. Thank you again for taking Salala and Bong Mines."

Nyenea watched the rebel and took in every word he uttered. He was most impressed with the rank given to Dekie and his job as the commander. He watched him carry his pistols strapped around his waist along with automatic machine guns every day. He admired Dekie. When Nyenea was left alone in his room, he would quickly get a gun and pretend to be Col. Dekie. "I'm going be just like him one day," Nyenea vowed.

Dekie noticed that his little friend was becoming hostile, but he kept quiet and decided to keep an eye on him. Nyenea started learning from Dekie's bodyguards to carry a gun and shoot. The gun was too heavy for him. All of the bodyguards liked him, and he decided to take advantage of the situation to get what he wanted, which was to become a fighter who would meet the rebel leader one day. *I'll shake hands and eat with him too.*

● ● ●

Dekie checked the big brown envelope and counted $100,000. "Wow! I'll be rich for the rest of my life! I wish I could bring my family back to enjoy it with me."

The country was plunged into a full-fledged civil war. By June, a large portion was controlled by the NPFL rebels. The rebels killed everyone who belonged to President Samuel Doe's Krahn tribe and the Mandingo tribe for supporting the president. Throughout Liberia, especially in Monrovia, schools were shut down. Normal life came to a halt as many families were now vulnerable to chaos and abuse. Many families started walking toward the hinterland from the cities as a showdown between the government and rebel forces in the capital became imminent. With 75 percent of the country now under the self-proclaimed president and rebel leader, life was not the same anymore.

Mr. Kiamu started contacting friends in Monrovia to get information about his sister and was told that Gibi had been taken over by the NPFL rebels. His news about the capture of Gibi that evening was very disturbing to the rest of the family. His parents were furious but tried not to show it to their granddaughters.

"Where could they be at this time when the rebels are literally destroying everything that lies in their path?" old man Sumo had asked. The girls did not take the news lightly as they had seen on all major news networks in the United States the scale of destruction in Liberia. They had spent most nights crying for their parents and Nyenea. Neneh had a dream one night; in that dream, the farm was destroyed, and she could not find their parents in the house. Her dream saddened the whole house that day. All the telephone lines within rebel territories were down. This made it extremely difficult contacting anyone within their control. They spent silent nights and days, trying to comfort one another.

Dekie started taking Nyenea along with him. He didn't like it, but he tried to please him after he insisted going out with him. Nyenea now got exposed to every form of violence. Dekie was not the person he'd known before. He learned every bad habit from his friend and big brother. Nyenea was considered Dekie's little brother by everyone.

Nyenea missed his parents very much, but he also felt confident and trusted his friend. He didn't know much about military ranks and how to head a rebel group. He only saw Dekie as his friend from their farm and nothing more. While other people who were old enough to be Dekie's father worshiped him and were willing to do anything he asked, Nyenea only saw Dekie as his friend. Dekie was pleased to see Nyenea adapt so fast without his parents.

They were in the car alone when Nyenea asked a question that left Dekie stunned to the bone. "When will I start training with you?"

Dekie was shocked but managed to stop the car abruptly. Nyenea instantly came forward and hit his head on the dashboard. He was not wearing his seat belt again.

"I'm sorry, Nyenea. I told you to strap on your seat belt. I didn't mean to hurt you but—"

"Is it because I talked about training that you stepped on the brakes?" Nyenea shouted.

Dekie tried to control his temper, but he lost it. "Do you want to fight, eh? Do you want to? I'll make you a child soldier!" That night, he thought that Nyenea might be right. *If I train him, he may be able to protect himself when I'm not around.*

• • •

Yeanue, Lulu, and Zowahbah started school in Danane. They were all school-mates. Yeanue told them about their brother and how nice he was to him.

"If it was not for your brother, I would have rotted in prison," Yeanue said. Lulu and Zowahbah were glad to hear something positive about their brother. "Our mom does not approve of him being a rebel soldier," Lulu said. They got home from school that afternoon and found another celebration going on in the house. A letter had arrived from the UNHCR's office. Saye's damaged kidney had removed and a new one transplanted.

"His health is fine, and he sends his greetings to all," his mother said in tears. The letter included a few photos that left everyone smiling and happy for him. "Thank God for my son. May God bless and keep him." Ma Yah thought about her son too and wondered where he was. She had given up on him joining them. *I knew he was lying when he talked about joining us later. If he continues, he will meet his fate.*

• • •

Mr. Mleh found it very difficult to cope with life under the rebels. He had witnessed gruesome and heinous crimes. His brother-in-law had told him about some, but what he saw was too terrifying for him to describe. The beheading of women and the use of their heads at the checkpoints, insertion of military knives into the vaginas of girls as young as five and six years; a nine-year-old boy having sexual intercourse with a woman between fifty and seventy years old.

There was no free movement. There were many checkpoints and harassments on a daily basis. He was asked about his tribe every time they went out to look at new refugees coming into Gbarnga. He had to speak his local Kpelleh language to confirm that he belonged to that tribe.

"Hey, you there! What is your name?" the rebels would ask.

"My name is Mleh."

"Which tribe are you from?"

"Kpelleh."

"Can you speak Kpelleh? What is your name?" A rebel would ask in Kpelleh. "My name is Mleh," he would answer in Kpelleh.

This was the routine every time he went out. Mr. Mleh thought about staying in Liberia to get his son, but he could not get a car to take him to Gibi. He gave in to his friend Mr. Varkpeh and decided to leave. Mr. Varkpeh knew a few of the rebel boys, so he paid $200 for them to hitch a ride to Ivory Coast. Mr. Mleh felt bad that he could not keep his promise to his dying wife to get their son out of Liberia. "You have to forgive me, Polan, but I can't stand another day here!"

Mr. Mleh felt his senses returning to a normal state as soon as they crossed the Logatou border and got into Ivory Coast. He felt as if he had just got out of hellfire itself with little demons carrying guns and knives to kill. They got to Danane in Ivory Coast at night and started looking for a place to stay. The UNHCR provided a temporary place for them until they could get a place of their own. The Ivorian government didn't provide a refugee camp for Liberians in Ivory Coast, and the UNHCR helped only in emergency cases. All the Liberians living there built or rented their own houses.

Mr. Mleh didn't have any money, and it made things a bit difficult for him. Many Liberians who could not afford houses to rent lived in churches. Mr. Mleh decided against calling his in-laws and his children because he didn't know what to tell them concerning his wife and son. Mr. Varkpeh tried to convince him but found it difficult. So, he backed away and kept the topic of his family out of their conversation. He gave some of his clothes and some pairs of shoes to Mr. Mleh. Every day that passed by, he thought Mr. Mleh was going to give up the ghost. He saw stress, depression, and loneliness in his friend.

One evening, Mr. Varkpeh informed him that he was going to travel to Ghana with a friend. "I'm sorry to leave you, but you can hustle on your own. Don't give up. Your daughters still need you. My family was murdered by the rebels, but I decided to go on with life. God will repay the perpetrators."

That night, Mr. Mleh thought of ending his life and joining his wife. He cried that night like a child.

● ● ●

Dekie and Nyenea trained daily. The child was quick to learn everything about the gun and asked many questions. The Beretta machine gun was smaller and easier to carry, so Dekie gave it to him. but Nyenea rejected it and instead went for the AK-47 rifle.

Dekie could not believe his eyes when he saw Nyenea carrying the gun on his shoulder like a trained soldier.

"Where did you learn how to carry that gun?"

"Your bodyguards taught me," Nyenea said. He turned and shot into a tree, expertly bringing down a dove.

Dekie stood with his mouth open. "Wow! My men really did well. So when I thought you were home away from the guns, you were with them. We'll keep up with our training for the next two weeks."

After two weeks of training, Nyenea was eager to use his gun. He went out with the most dangerous boys on the base one afternoon. They went on a looting spree without the consent of their commander. They got to a house where a fighter was selling a satellite dish. Nyenea instantly recognized it as theirs.

He called to one of the rebel fighters, "It's our dish, and I'm getting it from him." When they told the boy with the dish, he said that it was his and would not give it to anyone. Nyenea shot him in the head with everyone standing there. After that, he picked up the dish. "Take it to the house. It's mine!"

On their way back, everyone was silent and shocked by what happened. He showed no sign of remorse. He later saw a pregnant girl about his age. "Hey, come here! Why are you pregnant?"

The girl did not know what to say but starting crying. He slashed open the girl's stomach to see the child's sex. "She's carrying a girl-child, who will be useless just like her," Nyenea said. All his boys became scared of him that day. However, no one said anything about it to their commander. Not yet.

One evening, Nyenea met his bodyguards eating human hearts in pepper soup. "Did you kill a pig today?" Nyenea asked. No one said a word to him. He sat with them and ate. They all kept quiet. "Ah, I enjoyed the food. I'm going into the kitchen to get some more."

As soon as he left for the kitchen, all the boys argued among themselves. "We should have stopped him from eating." One of them said that Nyenea was capable of killing any of them without any reason. He had been there when Nyenea had killed the fighter over the satellite dish.

On reaching the kitchen, Nyenea went and took food from the pot. He ate the human liver and heart without knowing it, but he enjoyed the meal. It was his first of many meals. Nyenea started asking the boys to let him smoke marijuana with them. He soon became a pro after coughing on the first few drags. Nyenea became a cannibal like a lion. He often ate people's hearts and livers. He was drugged for most of the day.

Dekie sat down and thought about Liberia's Independence Day prior to 1990.

July 26, 1990, marked the first of many sad Independence Days to come in Liberia. He thought about how other African countries marked their independence as a day of freedom from their white colonial masters. The day is reflected on as a reminder of the people's oppression by their

European colonial masters. They gave speeches about those who died to liberate them. But in the case of Liberia, nothing is reflected on as a reminder of our freedom. The question that many Liberians failed to ask was this: Did we ever gain independence?

July 26, 1847, was believed to be the day that Liberians gained their independence. But from whom? As he thought about Liberia's independence in 1847, Dekie realized that the country's historians did not actually document the circumstances that led to independence. Other studies showed that the colonial masters (free slaves) in Liberia wanted to enjoy the paradise promised to them by the American Colonization Society and other societies that brought them to the shores of the Montserado River and Sierra Leone in 1822. Dekie rememembered reading that by the year 1906, nearly nineteen thousand freed slaves were resettled in what was now Liberia. They declared independence in order to constitute themselves as a legitimate republic. It was not independence for the indigens but for the free slaves to do business with the Western powers.

The mulattos, who were the products of black slave girls and their white masters, adopted the republic form of government from the United States in ruling Liberia. They ruled the indigens of the land in complete isolation from 1847 to 1860. There was no freedom or independence for the indigens even when the descendant of the freed black slaves ruled them from 1870 to 1980 under Edward James Roye, the first colored president of the True Wing Party (TWP).

The free slaves took over the indigens' land and named it Liberia. The capital city, Monrovia, was named for President James Monroe, who had been sympathetic to their repatriation. In 1819, an act was created to repatriate freed slaves back to Africa. The American national holidays such as Thanksgiving Day and the rest, had no meaning to the indigens but such traditions were adopted. The flag, seal, and national anthem reflect nothing of the people of the land, only of the United States. The freed slaves only thought of themselves and built a hegemonic rule that survived for 120 years without a revolt by the indigens.

The freed slaves came and found unity among the people of the land, but they distanced themselves from everything that had to do with the natives and their culture they deemed barbaric and demonic. The form of cultural unity deemed barbaric by the first freed slaves was recognized by their children more than a century later.

Many things linked the natives before the freed slaves arrived. One was the Poro and Sande societies popular among the Kpelleh, Dei, Kissi, Vai, Gbandi, and Lorma. These societies served to educate the tribal youths and promote unity among the ethnic groups. Extending from Gola, the Poro society used common rituals and languages to bind the different ethnic groups. They conducted a bush school that taught young boys and girls how to behave properly. *Our colonial masters are still dividing us*, Dekie thought.

In 1990, when many Liberians found themselves in displaced camps within their own country, it dawned on them that they were never free. The day arrived and passed without many people knowing that July 26 had come and gone.

Dekie shook his head for a long time. "Maybe our leader is right. We'll free our people." When Nyenea got to know that he had been eating human hearts and livers, it didn't bother him. Rather it hardened him, making him become like his boss. He got his first victim and removed his heart and liver.

"Take it and cook it at once!" Nyenea ordered the girls. At the age of fourteen, he looked like a baby, but he had gotten so wicked that even Dekie became careful with him.

"I'll be celebrating my birthday on January 1, 1991. My father said that he was going to buy me a motorbike and a stereo set," Nyenea told Dekie.

"I'll get them for you, and we have to get your parents' new pickup truck back too. I know who took it," Dekie said. He got a Yamaha motorbike and a Sony 3Disc stereo set for Nyenea and held a big birthday party for him. At the party, Nyenea took cocaine for the first time and went ballistic. Nyenea shot one of his bodyguards in the arm for refusing to pass him the marijuana. Dekie had to lock him up in his room to stop him from causing further trouble.

Nyenea was literally changing into something else, and everyone stepped aside when they saw him coming. He ordered Kamah to sleep with him. Kamah was only ten years old when she lost her virginity to him. Dekie tried to put a halt to it, but Nyenea questioned him about the twelve-year-olds that he was also sleeping with every night. At times, he got so high on drugs that his mind went blank, and he didn't know himself. Dekie stopped him from going out alone and banned his bodyguards from following him around. He decided to take Nyenea to the front lines in Monrovia and Robertsfield to teach him.

On the front line at the Robertsfield military base, Nyenea was at the front of the battle, shouting and advancing on the government soldiers without looking back. The rebel fighters feared for their lives, but not Nyenea. As long as he had enough cocaine in his system, he moved like a snake on his enemies. Dekie stood in shock as he saw his little boy move into one of the buildings. He followed him, and in no time, they came out with five government soldiers who had held them back there for hours. "Nyenea's bravery saved the day," Dekie said. The boy had learned every move from his commander and friend.

"You showed bravery out there today, my boy," Col. Dekie said and tapped him on his shoulder. After they captured Robertsfield Highway hilltop, Col. Dekie and his troops returned to base in Gibi.

"Gentlemen, let's give it up for Nyenea! He saved the day!" said Col. Dekie. His boys applauded for Nyenea.

That night, Kamah reported that one of the bodyguards had raped her when he was away. Nyenea called the boy out. "He forced me to sleep with him," Kamah said, crying. Nyenea took the girl and the boy behind the house and asked them to repeat what happened.

Dekie heard shots and ran out. He could not believe his eyes when he saw little Kamah and one of his boys dead in cold blood. Nyenea had shot them at close range, blowing their heads off. He asked his men to take the bodies away.

"Nyenea, go to your room and wait for me," Dekie ordered, furious.

"What happened?" Dekie asked as he met Nyenea in his room.

"He raped Kamah when we were out fighting," Nyenea said.

"But why did you also kill her?"

"I cannot eat another man's leftover," Nyenea said sarcastically.

Dekie could not get over the horrible changes he now saw in this kid from such a decent home. "Nyenea, you have to be careful, or someone will harm you in my absence. I heard about the boy you killed because of your satellite dish, and the pregnant girl."

"Yes, I know, but they should be careful with me too!" Nyenea said firmly and walked out of his room. Dekie could not speak as he stood there, staring at his back.

Nyenea never sat down to talk to anybody except Dekie. He had no one to play with except his boss. They would play games like Monopoly or UNO and share jokes, so he was afraid of going too far against Dekie.

December 1, 1990, was a sad day at the Baptist church in Danane. Mr. Mleh was buried by the pastor and the congregation after he committed suicide. He had taken poison and left a note for the pastor.

Pastor, please contact my daughters in the United States. Tell them that I failed and could not stand to tell them the truth about their mother and brother.

Along with other members of the congregation, Pastor Kollie was disturbed as he spoke at the funeral. "The war is destroying our lives and everything that we stand for as Liberians. Our brother took his life out of frustration. We never knew him, but we felt his pain after hearing his story." After the burial, the pastor decided to call Neneh to let the family know what had happened to their father. Mr. Mleh had lived in the church compound for six months. He had given up after the deaths of his wife and son.

After the Liberian peace talks failed in Geneva, Switzerland, and in Banjul, Gambia, the Economic Community of West African States

(ECOWAS), under the direct supervision of the Nigerian president Ibrahim Babangida and other ECOWAS leaders, set up an intervention force called the West African Peacekeeping Force to stop the bloodshed in Liberia. The force was commanded by a Ghanaian, Gen. Arnold Quinoo, who led the troops into Liberia, but the rebel leader rejected the intervention of the ECOWAS peacekeeping force. He sent Col. Dekie and his marines to attack them from the sea with rockets in order to prevent them from landing on Liberian soil, but they were overwhelmed by the massive force of the peacekeepers from their gunship. The peacekeepers had to launch missiles from their gunships to dislodge Dekie and his men. With the deployment of the peacekeepers in the city, they were mandated to enforce peace later by fighting anyone who attacked them.

On September 8, 1990, President Doe, his defense minister, the Special Security Service (SSS) director, and some of his ethnic Krahns left for the seaport in order to leave the country after he saw there was no way out of the crisis. Upon reaching the port, the field commander of the breakaway faction of NPFL and now head of the Independent National Patriotic Front of Liberia (INPFL) was called by an unknown caller to meet the president at the port. Many rumors had it that the American embassy called the field commander to kill the president. He and his rebel fighters overwhelmingly swept past the SSS, who guarded the president and entered without the intervention of the peacekeepers.

On reaching the floor of the ECOMOG commander's office, the president had no way out. "Mr. Doe, what are you doing in my territory?" the field commander asked.

"I'm visiting General Quinoo," President Doe had answered. He was shot in the leg at once and taken out of the office without any resistance from the general and the peacekeepers guarding his office. They stood still even when the president cried for help.

"Quinoo! Please help me!" President Doe cried. His hands were tied behind his back, and he was put in the trunk of his own limousine, which sped away to the field commander's base. The field commander stopped in New Kru Town, a suburb of the city, to display his catch to his many supporters. Some of the women poured dirty water on the president, saying, "You're a wicked man. You'll die like a dog!"

At the base, he was interrogated by rebels who had nothing to say but "Where's our money?"

"Cut off one of his ears! Maybe that will make him to talk," their commander had said. His ear was cut off, and Budweiser beer was poured on the fresh wound.

The president died the next day without anyone knowing the truth surrounding his death. Many Liberians believed that he was killed in retaliation for the death of the Nimbalians during his rule. After the death of President Samuel K. Doe on September 9, 1990, at the hands of Field Commander Gen. Yealue, the AFL seized power and installed its commander, David Q. Nimely, as the new head of state, pending the installation of the Interim Government of National Unity (IGNU) formed in Banjul, Gambia, by ECOWAS.

Nyenea and his squad stepped up her attacks on Monrovia in order to overrun the city and have full control of the country. The rebel leader's aim for the movement was not a partial control but a full presidential title as the president of the Republic of Liberia. But with the city now guarded by the West African Peacekeeping Force, it was impossible for the leader's dream to become a reality. Instead, they were pushed out of the city limits for a buffer zone created by a new commander, Gen. Rufus Kupolati from Nigeria.

The marines' base was now a fully established structure of the self-proclaimed rebel government. The rebel leader set up his government and appointed cabinet ministers. His controlled territory became like the old American Wild, Wild, West TV show. He tried hard to consolidate his hold on his territory, but it fast became increasingly fragile since the arrival of the West African Peacekeeping Force to stop the carnage.

The base became the most notorious training camps under the NPFL rebels. The base was used to commit atrocities, massacres, and anything that could push further their leader's goal of becoming president of Liberia at all costs. Col. Dekie's men were vicious and ready to go on all attacks. The cannibalistic practice of the group was one of the trademarks of the base. He and his men regularly ate human beings. Nyenea accused the guys who had taken his father's Nissan pickup truck and had killed them right on the streets of Kakata. His name reached the rebel leader after their success in Robertsfield. The rebel leader called Col. Dekie for a briefing and to inquire about Nyenea. "I've heard about your son. Is he really your son? We need young fighters to continue our struggle. But how old is he?" the leader asked.

"He's fifteen years old, but he's not my son, sir."

"What? So he's the 'child soldier' I have heard about. My goodness!"

"Yes, sir," Dekie answered.

"Bring him with you next month so I can have a word with him," the rebel leader said.

• • •

"Hello! Who's this?" Kaimu asked.

"I'm Pastor David Kollie from Ivory Coast. Please, may I speak to Neneh, Seanee, or Jokata?"

Kiamu instantly became attentive when he heard the words Ivory Coast. "I'm sorry, but they are all in school. I'm their uncle. You may leave a message for them."

"OK. Their father, Mr. Nuteh Mleh, died in our church premises a week ago. He wanted me to tell them about the deaths of their mother and brother in Liberia six months ago," Pastor Kollie said.

Kiamu was silent for a while before he could muster his courage. "Thank you, Pastor. I'm very grateful for your help. But how did he die?"

"He committed suicide," the pastor answered.

It took him sometime after his conversation with the pastor to place the phone down. He felt anger swelling up in him to hear about his only sister's death. He slowly turned to face his parents standing behind him. His parents had been standing there all that time, listening to the conversation. He could not lie to them.

"Who was that, and what happened?" his mother asked after seeing the expression on his face.

• • •

Saye called his mother and talked with the entire household. "I've started classes at the university here on scholarship. I'm studying mass communication to become a journalist. I was given political asylum by the US government, and I'm eligible to bring my family over."

"But I'm too old to come over in that cold weather. Let's see whether the girls and Yeanue can come over," Ma Kou replied.

"Have you people heard from Dekie yet?" Saye asked.

"No, we've not heard from him yet."

Saye asked to talk with Ma Yah. "How are you and the girls, Ma? Is my friend Dekie coming over?"

"We are fine. No, Saye. Dekie is fine with the NPFL. He has decided to be a rebel, and he's no longer a decent person."

"Yeah, but that place is not for him. He needs to get out, so I can bring him here to study. We planned to complete school together. Please say hi to the girls for me," Saye said.

He talked to Quianue and his wife before hanging up. He wanted to talk with Lulu but found it difficult to ask for her. After he hung up, he punched the air in frustration. *"I'm stupid for calling without talking to her. What was I thinking? She'll think that I'm a coward not brave enough to face her."*

Ma Kou, Ma Yah, Ma Norn, and her husband, Quianue, decided to stay in Ivory Coast and send their children to the United States for a better future. A month later, Saye filed for them and added Dekie's name to the list just in case he showed up. He also sent a letter to his friend Dekie.

By March 1991, Zowahbah, Lulu, and Yeanue left for the United States without Dekie. Ma Yah cried about Dekie's safety. She wanted him to leave the rebels and continue his schooling.

• • •

Nyenea met the rebel leader at his mansion in Gbarnga in March 1991. After the meeting, Nyenea was given the rank of lieutenant, and Dekie became a full general.

"General Dekie! It's good to see you after a year. I heard a lot about you from the president," Lt. Gen. Dudu said.

Dekie turned and saw a fake smile on his commander's face. "Yes, sir. I'm sure glad to see you too." Gen. Mosquito appeared from behind them with Lt. Nyenea.

"Ah, I see our child soldier is enjoying himself. I really thought he was your son until the president explained everything to me. I'm proud of you, boy. We're often regarded as nobodies, but we can make a nobody into somebody. You're now my comrade. From now on, don't regard me as your superior," Gen. Mosquito said to Gen. Dekie.

Dekie was the youngest general who had not trained outside Liberia. Later that night, he saw Lt. Gen. Dudu and Lt. Nyenea having a conversation. Before his troop left Gbarnga, he sent one of his boys, Jomo, to see his mother in Danane. He sent $20,000 to pay for their house rent and school fees. He also sent a letter to Saye with $5,000 enclosed.

He and Nyenea spent three days with the rebel leader and then left for their base. "Hey, I'm sorry that we've not found your parents yet, but we'll work at it together, OK? What do you think about our president?" Dekie asked Nyenea.

"He's cool. I think I like him. My father was wrong about him. His commanders are also cool," Nyenea replied.

"You're the youngest ranking soldier in NPFL, do you know that?" Dekie said.

"Well, I guessed so because I didn't see anyone my age at the program," Nyenea joked.

"What did you discuss with General Dudu?" Dekie asked.

"Nothing. He told me to be a good soldier, that's all," Nyenea said.

As soon as they got back to base, Nyenea became hostile to Dekie. Dekie noticed his actions but kept his cool.

"We have an operation to carry out inside Monrovia. The president wants us to waste a few people within the city by bombing certain targets with hand grenades. You'll head that special operation," Dekie said.

"When do we leave? Do you have a list of people for us?" Nyenea asked.

"You'll be in the city without being seen by the ECOMOG soldiers. Hit your targets and move out. You'll strike markets, bars, and crowded areas," he told Nyenea.

Civilians were allowed to travel from the rebel-held territory known as greater Liberia to and from Monrovia. Nyenea and his crew moved into Monrovia unnoticed by the peacekeepers. They camouflaged as civilians and entered the city. They struck targets in bars where no one noticed who came in and went out. They moved into very crowded markets and threw hand grenades that left many dead. Prominent and common citizens were hit. Grenades exploded in busy places and left scores dead. Monrovia became tense as many families mourned their lost ones. They traveled through the Paynesville pipeline and headed straight for the Fendell forest, where a car waited for them.

Nyenea sat in his room and stared at his sisters' picture in the gold frame. He had kept the picture on his table since he recovered it and a few family pictures from their house. Today was the first time that he had taken a good look at his sisters. He had not taken drugs for the two days since his arrival.

I have changed. What has come over me? He thought about his sisters and his parents for a long time. *Where are my parents? What has become of them?* Tears rolled down his cheeks. He thought of the day when he came home, thinking that his father was going to be angry with him for not asking permission before going out, and found his house destroyed and the warehouses in flames. He screamed before calling for some cocaine in order to sober up. He injected himself and smoked two joints of marijuana. This was his way of getting over his problems and avoiding reality.

Jomo, the boy sent by Dekie to his mother in Ivory Coast, returned with sad news. "The death of one Mr. Mleh was reported at the Baptist church in Danane. Your mom said that you should find out whether he's your new friend's father. Your sisters and Yeanue have traveled to the United States to live with Saye there. He went for medical treatment and got asylum from the US government. Here are the letters from Saye and your mother."

Dekie sat down, absorbing the bad news and the good. "Thanks for your help, Jomo. I really appreciate it. Please don't tell a soul about Mr. Mleh's death. He was Lt. Nyenea's father."

"Yes, sir!" Jomo said as he stood at attention before walking out.

Dekie was disturbed about the death of the man who had shown him so much love. He cried and stayed indoors for the rest of the day. "This war has brought total destruction to our lives, and I am one of the perpetrators. We'll all end up in hellfire! My friend Saye rejected everything that had to do with our madness, and he's now my sisters' savior. Oh, my friend Saye! Please forgive me one day!"

He opened the letter from his mother but didn't read it. He picked up his friend's letter with a very heavy heart and shaky hands. His heart pounded heavily as he scanned the sheet.

My dear friend Dekie,

I thank God for your life and all the people that God used to restore my health. I received a kidney transplant upon my arrival. I'm very grateful for your unwavering friendship. You're my best friend and will always be. We grew up knowing each other with lots of respect for each other.

Our plans for school and the future got disrupted by this senseless war, but you chose a path that no one around you supports. Let's make it up. Come to the United States, and we will fulfill our dreams. I'll be waiting for your arrival.

Truly yours, Saye

Dekie cried after reading the letter. "I can't come to the United States, my friend. I'm already a rich man with lots of cars, money, and girls at my disposal."

The next day, Dekie met Nyenea to discuss his father's death. "I'm sorry about what happened to your dad. You know, he was a father to me also. Let's stay together and see how we can get in touch with your sisters soon. The president is very proud of you, and he's going to promote you on his next trip here."

Nyenea didn't take in much of what his boss said because he was high on cocaine again. He sat there, looking at Dekie as if he was his enemy. His mind went to his discussion with Lt. Gen. Dudu during their trip to Gbarnga. Dudu had promised him $100,000 and Dekie's position as the base commander if he would kill his boss.

• • •

Saye was happy to see Lulu, Zowahbah, and Yeanue—especially Lulu. "Your family showed me so much love after your father found me in the forest," Saye said to Yeanue. They settled down quickly once he started processing their papers for green cards and to get them in school. "I heard that you all lived in Danane as a family. So we'll do the same here too."

Lulu and Saye had been secret lovers since when they were kids, and he always saw her as his future wife. Zowahbah knew all along that her sister was in love with Saye. *This may just be the right time for them to get married after finishing school*, Zowahbah thought. At seventeen, Lulu was very beautiful. She had won more than five beauty pageants since she was a child. Her dimples and slight space between her front teeth made her smiles beautiful to behold. Saye was beside himself since their arrival.

At twenty, he was smart and handsome, the only child of his parents. He opened the letter from his friend Dekie. When he didn't see Dekie at the airport, he had given up hope for his friend until he got a letter from him.

Dear Saye,

I'm very glad to write you. How's your health? Have you been to the hospital and if so, what was the result? I'm very concerned about your health. I know we don't agree on certain things, but we're still friends. I've chosen a wrong path that is going to haunt me all my life, but I think I've been nice to some people. Please fulfill our dreams by getting educated.

Yours truly, Dekie

Seanee, Neneh, and Jokata were very sad to hear about their parents' and Nyenea's deaths. They cried every day for a week. Everyone shifted the blame for their deaths onto Mr. Mleh. Ma Leneh was furious, but she had to comfort her grandchildren at the same time. It was hard for all of them, but the girls were more vulnerable. Their grandparents stopped shifting blame onto Mr. Mleh and started spending more time with them. After a month, the girls were now able to talk and watch TV. Kiamu found it very hard to forgive his dead brother-in-law for killing his lovely sister, Polan, and their only son. "I wish he had listened to me earlier. Man, he was so hard to convince about leaving his farm!"

The month ended with everyone silent about the girls' parents. It was too painful for all, so they agreed to drop the topic. Kiamu got scholarships for the girls to continue their studies. Neneh dreamed one night that she met Nyenea sitting in their house, alone. He never said a word to her. When she awoke, she told her sisters that their brother was still alive.

"I can feel him around me every time I sit alone. He is alive." No one doubted her, but they all kept quiet.

Nyenea soon forgot about his parents' death as he drugged himself daily. He was always high on one drug or another. Dekie came up to him for one dangerous assignment in Firestone Harbel. "We need to get the world's attention. So to do that, we have to strike hard at civilian targets. Go into the division as AFL soldiers, kill as many civilians as you can, and get out without being exposed as a member of our army." The operation was one of Nyenea's many barbaric genocidal campaigns.

Nyenea picked out his death squad from his previous trip to Monrovia. Strangely, he included Jomo. Nyenea had threatened Jomo since his return from Ivory Coast. Jomo had told the boys about Nyenea's father's death after Dekie had warned him not to.

Nyenea led the operation in the division, using a captured AFL truck. With their AFL uniforms on, they entered the division, a residential area of the Firestone Rubber Plantation Company. There were many displaced people all over the division. AFL and the ECOWAS peacekeepers controlled the division. So coming in an AFL truck made it easy for them to enter. Nyenea told his boys to kill as many people as they could get that night. They opened fire while the camp was quiet and everyone slept. People ran in every direction to escape. Nyenea and his thugs followed them into the rubber bush, shooting them down.

By two o'clock in the morning, before word could get out to the ECOMOG checkpoint ahead, the operation was over.

"Jomo, come over here," Nyenea called. Before Jomo got close to Nyenea, his colleagues were spattered with his brain. Nyenea killed him in cold blood with some of his friends standing by.

"Let's move it!" Nyenea shouted.

Back on the base, they were met by Gen. Dekie with lots of applause for a successful operation. "Well done, boys and our distinguished child soldier, Lieutenant Nyenea. The president will be here tomorrow to personally thank you all."

Later that night, it was reported to Gen. Dekie that Lt. Nyenea had killed Jomo after the operation. He was disturbed about Jomo's death. Jomo had been one of his most loyal rebels. But he was afraid to approach Lt. Nyenea about it because of the successful operation and the president's visit the next day.

The president's arrival was eagerly awaited by Nyenea. He also expected Dudu so that they could conclude their deal. He had finally decided to carry out the job. *I'll have this base to myself and can do anything that I want to do.*

The program was short as usual with lots of praises for Lt. Nyenea by the rebel leader. "This is our future defense minister. From now on, you're

Captain Nyenea!" He also appointed Nyenea as the deputy commander to Gen. Dekie of the marine base.

Dekie felt so proud of their achievement. *Only sixteen, and he is now a captain and close to the president. I guess we'll all be judged one day, but I think I've brought smiles to many.*

The rebel leader spent two days at the base, getting acquainted with his most dangerous loyalist. His visits didn't target civilians. He used sweet talk to stir up the suffering masses everywhere he went. He stopped by a group of civilians along the road to ask whether his men had been kind to them and used his most famous statement: "You're my pepper bush." The statement meant that he cared for them just as a farmer would care for his pepper farm in order to get a good harvest. He gained popularity and support from the grassroots to the so-called educated elites, who wanted to identify with the movement in hopes of a job.

Lt. Gen. Dudu and Capt. Nyenea secretly met to discuss their final deal. "When do you want me to get him out?" Nyenea asked.

"As soon as you're ready, you can strike. Just call me, and we'll meet in Kakata for your cash. I've already mentioned your assignment to the president," Lt. Gen. Dudu said.

"My son, your courage as a child soldier has made a great name for my movement. I need you to carry out a major assault on ECOMOG positions in and around the capital. Here's something for you," the rebel leader said and handed $50,000 to Nyenea.

"Thank you, sir. I promise to do my best."

After the rebel leader's departure, Dekie held a birthday party for Nyenea. Nyenea had totally forgotten about his birthday. Dekie celebrated the new year and Nyenea's birthday together. All the fighters at the party came with lots of teenage girls, who had been forced from their homes and raped several times.

When Nyenea heard the birthday song, it sank into him. "So today is my birthday? I can't believe it." Dekie knew that he had forgotten and decided to surprise him. Everyone clapped at the end of the song. Nyenea was congratulated on his birthday, his new post, and his promotion to the rank of captain. He sat there looking at everyone who came by to shake his hand. After the party, he took one of the fighter's girlfriends just as the girl was about to enter the fighter's car.

"Hey! Get out of that car!" Capt. Nyenea commanded the girl. He took her away without the boyfriend saying a word. No one on the base messed with him. Nyenea was ruthless and as dangerous as an African python. He killed without hesitation.

"What's your name?"

"Tina," the girl answered. She seemed a lot older than him. The girl was twenty years old.

"Where did you live before the war?" This was the most popular question now in Liberia. Everyone found themselves in one place or another within the country. Civilians ran from their homes; they found themselves migrating all the time.

"I lived in Bong Mines."

"Where, to be precise?"

"Bong Town Golf Club."

"Which school did you attend there?"

"I graduated from Bong Town High School. Why are you asking? Do you know Bong Mines?" Tina asked.

"I'm a former student of that school, but my sisters graduated from there."

"Wow! I'm so glad to meet someone from Bong Mines and my former school." She was smiling now and relaxed with him until Dekie came in.

"Excuse me, please. Hi, Tina. Captain, join me," Dekie said and kept on walking. Nyenea asked the girl to wait for him.

"What are you doing? That girl is my friend's wife. Why did you order her out of his car? Nyenea, I told you to be careful here. I'll have to send you somewhere else!"

Every rebel fighter was married as long as he had a girl in his home. On hearing about his removal from the base, Nyenea said, "I'm sorry. Please take her away."

Back in the living room, Tina saw the opportunity to have this kid around her little finger. Her boyfriend, Lt. Johnson, had more than a hundred other girlfriends. *He's charming, young, and more educated than that good-for-nothing that I'm wasting my time with. I'm going to stay right here.* Many of the young girls were out of their homes, and many parents were dead or displaced. They used their bodies as a means of survival.

Gen. Dekie called the girl outside. "I'm taking you to Johnson's house."

"No! I'm not going there. I'm tired of the abuse. In fact, I love Nyenea."

Dekie was shocked to hear his friend's girlfriend say this. "Well, if you say so, but I want you to know that you'll be pitting my soldiers against one another."

Nyenea joined them later.

"Well, my captain, please take Tina in, but remember that you'll be at war with Johnson from now on."

The news about the marine base commander was not a surprise to Ma Yah. She had known that her son had decided to take the path of evil. From that day, she vowed not to take any money from him again.

"That's blood money!" Ma Yah said.

Gen. Dekie's marine base had gained a reputation for murder, cannibalism, and the rape of young and old women. The name "General Dekie" shocked Ma Yah. "How can he be a general when he's not even a high school graduate or a soldier, for that matter? He's just a child, and children are being used by these wicked demonic leaders to further their evil acts against the Liberian people. My son is not a general!"

She had always loved her only son. Her son had had plans of going to school and becoming someone respectable in society. Her pains eased as the news of her daughters' progress in school got to her. On the phone, she was so happy to talk to her daughters. The three families shared a deep sense of oneness. With their children now in school, they hoped for a brighter future. Lulu and Zowahbah had always wanted to be medical doctors and save lives and now, it would be possible for their dream to come true.

Saye cried all night after reading Dekie's letter. It pained his heart that his friend had refused to change even after realizing the evil truth about the war. "He's killing his own people and destroying Liberia without any sense of remorse," Saye said. He had asked Yeanue about his time with the movement, and there was nothing positive about it. *But they have not thought once about the destruction of their own country and their lives. Yeanue rejected everything and is now safe with a better future. I stood against them and was willing to give up my life. Those people are evil. If Liberians stay, they're just going to remain at the border without going anywhere! Oh, I wish my friend would listen to me.*

Dekie felt hurt after reading his friend's letter, but he found himself moving away from the truth and reality of his loved ones, including his own family and best friend. He started thinking about backing away, but how could he do that after accomplishing much in just a short time? He had enough cash and more than ten good cars. He had gained respect from his peers, including the rebel leader. He thought hard of his small friend, Nyenea and how he had changed within a very short time. He could carry out any operation without a trace.

"I can't walk off just like that. This is my destiny," Dekie said.

Nyenea and Tina now lived together. "I graduated with one Seanee Mleh in 1988. Do you know her?" Tina asked.

"She's my older sister," Nyenea answered.

"Are you Nyenea, their brother? But you were so small at that time. Now we're sleeping together."

"Well, I'm a man now. My sisters are in the United States, and our parents are dead. I'm the only one here in Liberia," Nyenea replied.

"Oh, I'm so sorry to hear about your parents. My parents got killed in Bong Mines too by the field commander," Tina said.

"I'm also sorry about your parents' death," Nyenea said. Since Tina moved in with him, he had not taken any cocaine or booze for two days. He went to work regularly. He was trying to be nice to Tina, showing some manners. But how long could he keep up the pretense?

Capt. Nyenea was responsible for carrying out all the deadly operations for NPFL. In his office, he was responsible for planning all the dirty jobs, from genocide to causing havoc within cities and towns, meant to provoke the international community into getting involved with the conflict and bring about a ceasefire. These acts also delayed the pressure from the peacekeepers and other factions' assault on the NPFL positions. With new war fronts opened in Firestone, fifteen gate, Todee, and the arrival of a new rebel movement from Sierra Leone, the rebel control of the country was now less than 70 percent. There was a major obstacle to the movement's success now that ECOMOG became a peace enforcer. The rebel leader gave orders for all West African immigrants within his controlled areas to be assassinated on the grounds that ECOMOG was one of his movement's enemies. Hundreds of Ghanaians, Nigerians, Guineans, and Sierra Leoneans were murdered in cold blood, and hundreds more were imprisoned. Teachers from these countries were found everywhere in Liberia, working for US dollars.

"Captain, we've learned that there are many Nigerians, Ghanaians, and Sierra Leoneans living in Bong Mines. I want you to get there and kill them all, including their hosts," Dekie instructed him. Nyenea and his death squad moved into Bong Mines that night. They went around and made inquiries.

"I know many of them were teaching in Bong Community High School in Varney's Town. So, let's find a student from there to tell us their whereabouts," Nyenea told his squad. Many of the teachers from West African countries were killed. The rest ran into the bush for safety. Some students volunteered to escort them from Bong Mines through the forest to Loffa and Bomi Counties. Nyenea and his squad killed many small-trade businessmen and their hosts.

Nyenea picked up his Motorola walkie-talkie. "General Dekie, the town is already zero. We're going into Kakata to check out the city. Over." After two days of terror, the residents were relieved when Nyenea left. The rebels had gone from house to house, searching for teachers and business-people. They killed many people in the town and returned to their base, leaving countless families devastated. They killed every friend and associate of West African immigrants. Mandingos who had lived in Liberia for many years as citizens were killed. The mention of Nyenea's name made civilians run into hiding. Captain Nyenea became the most feared and dangerous young rebel in the NPFL movement.

The base tactics were dangerous, but their leaders saw them as the best. Against this background, they started planning a major attack meant to overrun Monrovia and cause damage and havoc in the city. The code name "Octopus" came into play. Gen. Dekie and Capt. Nyenea and other commanders were involved in planning for this major operation. They were to enter Monrovia from all sides and push the ECOMOG troops out of the city. The city now had an interim president, Dr. Amos Sawyer. The NPFL showed their greed for power. The rebel leader didn't go just to oust the late president, he also went to hijack power and rule by any means.

Capt. Nyenea was on active duty with his commander. The push for devilish acts became music for all of them. Their commander tried to minimize civilian casualties, but all the operations were geared toward the destruction of the civilian population. They moved quickly at any opportunity to strike against civilians and kill as many as possible. Dekie wanted someone else for the job, but Nyenea was so furious about it that he dropped it. Dekie always looked at him in amazement. *I know deep within me that my own boy can erase me without a trace.* The thought was horrible, but he had taught him every evil thing in the book.

Nyenea became a sadist. Every time he had sex with Tina, it was punishment for her. He would get so high on cocaine that he cried for help after every sexual encounter. She was afraid of him most of the time. She saw the devil in him, but he looked so young and innocent. He didn't talk much. He used to laugh with his friend Dekie, but that had stopped a long time before.

"I want to go to Ivory Coast to see my younger sister. I heard she's there with some friends. I'll also bring her over," Tina said one day.

"When do you want to go?" Nyenea asked.

"Next month. September."

"I'll want you to buy me some provisions. Just tell me when you're ready." He walked away without another word.

He had lots of respect for Tina and saw her as one of his kind. He decided to move back to his father's house and clear and rebuild farmland. A team came from Kakata to renovate the entire farm. He also got the rebel leader's interior designer to redesign the house.

Dekie was happy to see some changes in his boy after his decision to move back home. "Tina, you're amazing. You brought my boy back to his senses. He has never been like this," he said to Tina. Nyenea kept to himself; he was sick of the crowd in Dekie's house. That was why he left. As far as Tina was concerned, he was still the same wicked small soldier.

"I want you to move in with me. I want the two of us and my bodyguards to be on the farm," Nyenea said to Tina. Tina was from the city. She knew and enjoyed everything civilized. Her looted clothes showed class and style.

Nyenea and Tina moved into the house in September. The house was built in the style of Bong Mines houses, and this made her comfortable. He had four cars—the rebel leader had given him a Land Rover jeep, and Dudu had given him a brand-new Ford pickup truck. He also had his father's car and another Nissan patrol jeep from Dekie. Tina was given the Land Rover jeep to use with two bodyguards. He got James, his rescuer, to take care of the farm along with other hired workers. Tina looked through his family pictures. She knew the family very well. The pictures of her friends made her cry as she thought of them now in the United States. She came across a recent picture of them standing in the snow. At the back of the picture, there was an address and a telephone number. She copied down the phone number.

Nyenea gave Tina $15,000, some bodyguards, and the jeep to travel in. Dekie met her that morning and gave her $10,000 for his mother and $5,000 for the other families. Tina had a smooth ride with a pass and the rebel escort provided by Dekie. Knowing the kind of men under their banner, he provided enough security. The escort stopped at the border in Logatou and waited for her return. The rebels were allowed to travel in Ivory Coast with their cars but not with their guns. Tina's bodyguards left their guns at the border and crossed in their jeep—something that had everyone staring at them.

In Danane, they slept in a motel and located Dekie's mother the next day.

"Hello, Ma. My name is Tina. I brought you a letter and some money from your son, General Dekie. I also have some money for Ma Kou and Mr. Quianue," said Tina.

Ma Yah stood for a long time, staring at the young girl in disgust. "I don't have a son by that name. Please get out of here before I call the gendarmes to arrest you."

Ma Kou heard the noise and ran out. She found her friend standing with an expensively dressed young girl. "What happened?"

"I brought a letter for her from her son, General Dekie," Tina said.

"Take the letter and go inside, Yah," Ma Kou said.

Ma Yah took the letter from Tina and was about to enter when Tina said, "I have some money for you also."

Ma Yah instantly turned around and said, "Take his money back to him! I do not need his blood money anymore!"

"Excuse me, Ma. I also have some money for Mr. Quianue and Ma Kou."

Ma Kou wanted to take the money, but one look from her friend made her turn her back, and they went inside.

"I'll be at the motel on UN Street. You may come and see me if you change your mind," Tina said and got in her car. She sped off hurriedly to avoid further disgrace as many people had come around to see who was riding in such an expensive car. Only NPFL rebels were seen with such cars in the town.

Mr. Quianue and his wife got home and met a lot of onlookers at their house. Both women were sitting quietly, staring at the walls. The TV set was off.

"Why are those gossips standing outside our house?" Quianue asked.

"Dekie sent a girl here to see us, and I drove her away. I've decided not to take any money from him again. He also sent some money for you all if you want it. You may pick it up from her where she's staying—at the motel on UN Street," Ma Yah said.

"We can't take money from him as long as you don't approve of it. After all, we also don't approve of this senseless war against our nation," Quianue said.

Tina learned later that her sister had moved to Maim, which was an hour's drive from Danane. She didn't see anyone from Ma Yah's house that night until she left to find her sister. She wondered why Dekie's mom refused the money. There were many people who wish for such an opportunity.

She met her sister, who was living with a boy. Rita was taken from the boy's house to the hotel.

"You're not staying here with that fool. I'm taking you back with me tomorrow."

"I'm not going back to Liberia. Our parents got killed there, and we were left to fend for ourselves in that godforsaken country. I'm not going back there. You send me to either the United States or Europe."

Tina had tears in her eyes when her little sister reminded her of their parents' death. She had been present when the rebels had killed their father and their mom was raped by ten horrible-looking rebels who had not bathed in months. Their mother had died a week later due to lack of medication for her infected wounds. She and her sister had escaped to Kakata and gotten mixed up with hundreds of people. She later heard that her sister was seen in Ivory Coast. Tina loved her sister dearly. She cried out loud when she could not hold it in any longer. "OK, I'll help you to get out by any means, but promise me that you'll come with me to Abidjan so we can spend few days together." They hugged, crying.

Tina left her bodyguards at the motel in Danane. Her driver was an elderly man, and she bought some clothes and shoes for him. He looked like a real gentleman in his new suit. They spent three days in Abidjan shopping and having fun. Rita was the prettier of the girls with a beautiful smile that left men wanting more.

"Look, Rita, I'm not OK with this life either, but I am with someone who cares for me. Oh, I almost forgot. I have to call my friend Seanee in the United States."

"How's their brother, Nyenea? I had a crush on him when we were in school. We were classmates, remember?" Rita asked.

"Yeah. Look, Rita. Nyenea is not the kid you once knew. He's the deputy commander on the marine base in Gibi, and he's my boyfriend."

Rita went mad on hearing that her older sister had snatched her long-time secret lover. "It's not fair for you to take him away from me!"

"You can go back with me and have him, or stay here and keep quiet!" Tina said firmly.

● ● ●

Nyenea missed Tina very much. He had taken up with her because of his needs. Sex was still new to him. He decided to go back to drugs in order to keep his mind off her, but it was impossible. He spent more time at Dekie's house before coming home after work. The poultry and piggery had picked up again. James was doing a great job in keeping the place alive. There were many workers at the farm working for food as wage. They were paid with rice weekly.

There were no jobs. People would do anything just to feed their families. The farmers could not farm because they were afraid of the rebels, who not only would take the products, they would also destroy everything. The rebel leader sent enough rice to feed his fighters and to keep them well fed for the killing to continue. Nyenea used his rice ration to feed his workers.

● ● ●

"Hello? May I speak to Seanee?"

"Who is this?"

"My name is Tina from Liberia."

"Is this Tina from Bong Mines?"

"Yes."

"Oh, Tina! This is Neneh."

Tina and Neneh were not too close because they both had a crush on the star basketball player in their school, but neither of them thought about it now as they talked, trying to catch up on all the happenings. "Seanee is not in now."

"Oh, that is fine. Let's keep talking. I'm sorry about your parents' death, Neneh."

"Yeah, thanks. Our little brother, Nyenea, was also killed by the rebels."

Tina was shocked to hear that. After a pause she said, "Nyenea is not dead. In fact, I've just been at his house on the farm in Gibi."

The noise from the other side made Tina hold the receiver away from her ear. "What did you say, Tina? We received a call confirming his death in December last year."

"No, he's not dead. He celebrated his sixteenth birthday in January."

Neneh finally knew that their brother was still alive and well.

Tina heard Neneh shouting. "Nyenea is alive! Our brother is alive!"

"Hello, Neneh! Are you there?"

"Hi, pal."

Tina instantly recognized her friend's voice. "Hey, Seanee! What's up, my girl?"

The joy and excitement in Seanee's voice was just too much for Tina. They talked for the next thirty minutes.

"So, where's our brother?" Seanee asked.

"He is on your farm in Gibi. He's a captain in the army and the deputy commander for the marine base in Gibi."

Seanee could not believe what she heard. "I'll call in two days," Tina said and hung up.

The house was still celebrating the news when Kaimu returned from work. He noticed that the mood in the house was different from what he'd known in the past two months. Everyone ran to greet him with the good news.

"Nyenea is alive! We got a call from Seanee's friend today in Abidjan. She's from the farm in Gibi," Ma Leneh told Kiamu. This was the best news that the house had gotten since the sad news from Pastor Kollie.

"What can we do to get him out of there? Is he all right?" Kiamu asked.

"Yes, Uncle. My friend said that he's fighting for the NPFL rebels as their deputy commander on one of their bases. I think she said the marine base," Seanee said.

"I'll call friends in Monrovia to confirm the existence of the base in Gibi tomorrow. We have to draw up a strategy to get him out. He's too young to be with such a devilish group. They've turned all of our small boys into child soldiers."

"Kiamu, please try and get him out of that place," old man Sumo urged his son.

Kiamu called a friend in Monrovia and got terrible news for the family. "My friend said that they're the most feared base in the country. Their leader is one General Dekie Woodor, a high school dropout from BWI. It's also difficult to get by their gate on the Salala highway. Suppose we ask your friend to get him out for us since she stays with him," Kiamu suggested to Seanee.

The phone rang, and everyone rushed to answer the call.

"It's yours, Uncle," Jokata said.

Kiamu hung up after a five-minute discussion with his friend in Monrovia. "My friend said it's impossible for him to go in. It's also true that our little Nyenea is the deputy commander of the base."

The house was silent for about five minutes as everyone thought about what they'd heard. Then the phone rang again.

"Yes, this is Seanee."

"Hey, Tina! How are you again? How's your sister, Rita?"

"She's fine. We're here together."

"Oh, I see. How is she? My regards to her. So we are now without parents." Seanee said.

"Yeah, I guess so. How's your school?" Tina replied.

"I'm in my final year. I hope I'll be completing my BSc next year, Look, T, I would like you to do me a favor." Seanee called her T only when she needed something. Tina had not forgotten, so when she heard her nickname, she knew what was next.

"We're friends, so just tell me what you want, and I'll gladly be of service," Tina said.

"We want our brother to come over to the United States. Can you get him over to Ivory Coast so we can speak to him?"

"Yeah, that's going to be a difficult one for me, but I'll try. You see, your brother is not the kid you left behind in Bong Mines. He has a lot of money and so much authority. It will be very difficult to convince him to come here or travel to the United States." There was a pause before Tina continued. "Your brother has four modern cars, twenty bodyguards, and servants who literally worship him." Tina thought she was boasting about Nyenea's wealth to his sister, but she was destroying him instead.

To the family in the United States, Nyenea was still their baby brother who needed education, not a rebel in the bush for some unscrupulous, sick, and mad rebel leader.

Tina hung up and sat down, thinking about the task of convincing Nyenea. She knew it was a Herculean task, but she could not say it to her friend. She would not understand.

Rita saw the look of frustration on her sister's face and knew that something was wrong.

She paid $1,500 for Rita to travel with a family to the United States as their sister under their family name. This was a common practice among the refugees. You could buy a name from a family and emigrate as one of them. Your name as well as your age would be changed. You would have a new identity. Rita and her new family were to leave in January 1992.

Nyenea thought a lot about Tina. He had a mission to kidnap two or more ECOMOG soldiers from Fifteen Gate on Monrovia highway. He had declined because his thoughts were not on fighting. He missed Tina. She had taken a great portion of him since their meeting.

"Is she coming back, Dekie? I really miss her."

"Tina is going to return. She's having a great time here with you. Look, you're still young. Just take it easy for now. If she's not coming, your boys will bring the news back," Dekie said.

CHAPTER 6

• • •

LULU AND SAYE WENT OUT for the first time. Everyone kept to his corner. They ate in silence and kept their distance.

"How did you feel the day I took you home after you fell?" Saye asked. Lulu hated to think about that day. She had felt humiliated before everyone, especially Saye. At the age of five, she'd had her eyes on him. She saw him as her brother's good friend. He and her brother spent time together at their house, but he never paid attention to her until that horrible rainy day when she fell in the mud.

"I hate that day," Lulu said flatly.

"I fell in love with you when you won the second-grade beauty pageant. You were awesome parading before the judges," he said.

"I always thought of myself as a born queen. I was fifteen years old and ran as the youngest queen in our high school in 1989 and won without you saying anything to me. We are very grateful to you for getting us here to the United States. My sister and I can now complete our education," Lulu replied. "Yes. We all can complete our education. I want to ask you a personal question. Do you miss Dekie?"

"We do miss him a lot, but he has decided to leave us and be with the rebel leader. Our mother doesn't want us to worry about him anymore, but it's difficult not to think of him."

"I love you, Lulu." Saye held her hand on the table. Lulu felt her face grow hot and pale. As they held hands, she felt her body get so warm that she could not bear it any longer. She pulled her hand back. These were the words that she had always wanted to hear from this handsome young man. Her heart beat fast, and sensations washed over her.

Is this how strong love is? "I've always loved you, Saye!" She then placed her hand over his.

● ● ●

Tina's arrival brought relief to Nyenea. He quickly sent his bodyguards to Kakata for a load of booze for an all-night party. Dekie and most of the high ranking rebels—except for Lt. Johnson—were at the party. The party lasted all night as everyone danced and enjoyed themselves. The next day was a quiet one. They woke up in the late afternoon with the sun shining on the porch. Nyenea tried to catch up on the details about Tina's trip.

"My trip was fine, and my sister and I had a wonderful time together. I brought some pictures of her."

"I missed you so much, Tina, that I don't think I'll allow you to travel again. Thanks for bringing my soap and deodorants," Nyenea said.

"You're always welcome," Tina replied.

"Why didn't you bring your sister? Do you know that we used to be pen pals?" Nyenea asked.

"She wants to go to the United States for studies. I think you two were more than pen pals because she was in love with you," Tina said.

"Oh, everyone is going to the United States nowadays. Will you leave me too for the United States? Well, don't be jealous of Rita; you have me all to yourself."

"I'll stay here with you if you promise to always love me."

He laughed out loud and said, "I promise to always love you." He thought about his statement and how foolish it sounded to him.

Tina thought about how to bring up the topic of Nyenea's sisters to him. As they sat outside, she decided it was the right time to bring it up. "Would you like to talk to your sisters someday?"

"Yes. They are my sisters, and I love them very much."

Tina asked the question in another way. "Would you like to see them or visit them?"

"Yes. I'd like to see them again."

Tina's heart skipped a beat as she listened to him.

"But why are you asking me these questions?"

"It's normal that your sisters and your grandparents would be concerned about you. Why don't you try to contact them, at least?" Tina asked.

"I don't have their phone number. My parents had it, but I never asked them for it."

"We could check for it and try to call," Tina said.

"Yeah, I think I miss them too. Look, thanks for your concern but we'll do that another time after you rest from that long ride."

• • •

The first Christmas party for Saye's guests became emotional as they geared up for the day. The winter was too cold for all of them. There were lots of purchases to be made and calls to Ivory Coast. They called their parents and finally, Saye told his mother about his love for Lulu.

His mother was very excited to hear the news. "I always knew that you two were made for each other." He also talked to Ma Yah and Mr. Quianue and his wife. Ma Yah told him about her decision concerning Dekie.

• • •

Nyenea sat and listened to Tina. "Did she explain why she did not take the money from you?"

"Yes, she said it's blood money."

"I'll give him the cash back and explain things to him. Maybe his mother is just angry with him for being a freedom fighter. He told me about his friend Saye and how he refused to be a soldier and almost got himself killed."

• • •

"General, we have to talk."

Normally when Nyenea addressed Dekie like that, it meant danger, so Dekie prepared himself for anything as his boy went on.

"Tina brought your money back. She said your mother refused to accept it. She called it 'blood money,'" said Nyenea.

Dekie sat as if he had just gotten a bullet in his head from his boy. He took the money from Nyenea and put it on the table. "I know she's listening to Saye! Damn you, Saye!" He burst into tears as if his body was being lowered into the grave from the shot. Nyenea could not believe the sight of his general crying like that.

"Look, Nyenea. I tried to tell you from the very beginning to leave the country and join your sisters in the United States. My family and my best friend have excommunicated me because of my involvement in this war. This war is against our own people. The reputation of this base is terrible, and we are feared all over the country. I didn't want to continue in this war, but because of greed, I held on, and now my mother doesn't want to accept me or my money anymore."

There was silence for a while before Nyenea spoke. "I'm sorry, Chief. It was after they killed my parents that everything changed for me. I'll stand by you!"

Dekie was pleased to hear his boy say that he would stand by him. With his family and his friends now estranged from him, he saw little Nyenea as his only friend and companion. He didn't trust Nyenea, but he felt better after talking to him. "I have to live my life and forget about what others think about me," Dekie said.

Nyenea thought about his boss and friend and could not get over the fact that his mom could reject him. *Is this how my father would've reacted?* How could they forsake him at a time like this? They should come and enjoy his riches. Nyenea and many others got involved in the crisis without knowing who the enemy was or why they fought in the first place. They saw the looted goods as riches and killed the owners indiscriminately. They only saw the war as a way to gain and what they could achieve. From the leaders down to the cannibals, they had enriched themselves with other people's property, whether it belonged to companies or individuals.

"I'll not leave all of this for the United States. If my sisters want to see me, they should come here."

"Tina, please go to Ivory Coast and call my sisters to come and spend the Christmas holiday here on our farm. I want you to leave tomorrow. I found the number behind their picture. If they can't come now, they should prepare to come for New Year's," Nyenea said. Tina had already thought about traveling back to Ivory Coast to buy some things for Christmas, so this was a perfect time.

Dekie came over that night and gave some money to Tina to buy a few things for himself and his girlfriend, Musu. Musu was his latest catch. He wanted to send some cash to his mom, but the first humiliation was still fresh in his mind. He felt bad for not being the one to support his mom. He always thought of her and his sisters as his responsibility. He cried on his way back to his house. He felt the loneliness deeper than ever before. He wiped away his tears as he got closer to home so that he would not be seen by his girlfriend Musu. Since the news from his mother, he felt empty. At first, he thought he could get over it, but nothing could fill the gap that he felt inside. *Will I ever see my mom again?* He knew the answer to his question, but he wasn't willing to face it.

He had gone too far from all his loved ones to turn back. If he ran away from the rebel movement, he would be hunted down, and Ivory Coast was not the best place for hiding. The NPFL leaders used the country as their backyard and rented the most expensive houses, and they had a security network that was capable of tracking anyone from anywhere.

Monrovia was another place, but he risked being arrested by ECOMOG soldiers. The only option was to sneak to Ivory Coast and then to Ghana and move on to any country of his choice. He had not been barred from entering Ivory Coast, but he could not desert the movement and live there.

Tina traveled with the same bodyguards and an escort to the border. December 15, 1991, was a bright sunny day in Danane. Many Liberians crowded the little town. The town had almost doubled in population as Liberians crossed the border to safety.

She met Rita that night and took her to the motel where she was staying.

"How's your resettlement program?" Tina asked.

"We'll be leaving on December 29. But sister, I've been thinking about you also. Why don't you leave that bush? Our parents would never approve of such a life. Our aunt will want to know why you are staying behind," Rita said.

Rita's question came as a shock to Tina. She never thought about her own future. She was caught up in the short-term riches of the movement. She and the rest did not know where the money came from, but they went on partying.

That night, Tina called Nyenea's family. "Hello, this is Tina from Liberia."

"Hey, Tina! How are you doing?" Seanee asked.

"I'm fine, my girl. What's up? Your brother sent me to inform you that you all should come and spend the Christmas holiday with him on the farm."

Seanee's throat went dry as she choked, "What? Are you serious? We want our brother out of that horrible place, and he's asking us to come there? I can't believe you said that!"

"I am not the one who suggested this, Seanee, but your brother is not willing to leave Liberia now. He's a soldier with thousands of men under his control. He said if you guys can't make it now, you can come for the new year."

"We need him out of Liberia, Tina!" Seanee sobbed. She could not bear the idea of their brother not coming to them.

Ma Leneh overheard the conversation and came over to take the phone from Seanee. "Hello, this is Nyenea's grandma. Please help us get him to Ivory Coast."

"Hello, Grandma. I wish I could do that, but your grandson is not the person that you knew before you left Liberia. I've talked to him, and that's why I'm here again. I'll call tomorrow, Ma," Tina said and hung up.

Nyenea had made his decision and wasn't going to back down. Tina knew, but she wished she could make his family understand. Her task was a very difficult one as she thought of how her friend felt about her. *I hope Seanee will not blame me someday for not doing much to encourage her brother to join them.* She started thinking about Dekie's mother and her actions. Now her childhood friend would complete university while she was not even thinking about school. *Are we not seeing the reality of this war?* She lay in her bed, thinking, until she dropped off to sleep.

"I want to go in and get him out of that godforsaken bush where they're murdering and destroying the lives of children. I'll get him out, Mom! I'll wait for Seanee's friend to call so we can discuss it further," Kiamu vowed. The excitement in the house was now dying down as everyone found it impossible to believe Tina.

"Maybe she's telling us the truth after all. Let's wait for her call," old man Sumo cautioned. Tina called, and they made arrangements for Kiamu to travel to Ivory Coast. Tina promised to pick him up from the airport in Abidjan and take him over to Nyenea.

• • •

Saye's house bubbled with the Christmas activities. That was nothing compared to the Christmas week with shopping going on through the city. The city was lit up with all kinds of Christmas lights. Saye enjoyed the look on the faces of his guests. "I had the same look last year. It is awesome to behold. We live in poverty while the West is basking in wealth, and our leaders don't care. We have a rebel leader destroying our nation while these people are moving forward."

They celebrated Christmas quietly. Saye said it was not good pretending to be happy while their people suffered. "I'm glad that all of you are here today. We thank God for his goodness and mercies toward us. But let's remember our dear Liberia as we celebrate the day."

Everyone understood what Saye meant and did as he said. They made phone calls to their parents to find out how they were celebrating.

• • •

Nyenea and his commander had a joint Christmas party. All the rebels on the base ate and drank until they could no longer handle another mouthful. Nyenea thought about his uncle coming for New Year's Day instead of his sisters. He didn't know his uncle, and the last picture he'd seen of him was from a long time ago. *I don't want to see him. He's coming to get me out of my base. It can never be. I'm fine here and will remain here.* Tina had promised to leave the country as soon as she got enough money from him.

Kiamu planned his trip to Liberia and did not know what to expect. He had seen pictures of Nyenea and an old photo of Tina. He had left Liberia over sixteen years before, in 1975. He had wanted to meet Nyenea in Ivory Coast, but his nephew insisted that he would not leave Gibi. He called his friend from Monrovia to inquire about movements in the NPFL territory. His friend's advice was that he (Kiamu) should remain in Ivory Coast and not bother going in. Kiamu's mother was not happy about that and had insisted that he go in and get her grandson out. He contacted the American embassy in Monrovia for information about going into the rebel held areas, but he was told not to try it; it was suicide. Against all odds, however, he decided to get his nephew out.

Tina came with her usual team of armed guards to pick Kiamu up at the airport. In two days, her sister would leave for the United States. She first called Seanee, who confirmed Kiamu's departure for Ivory Coast. Tina and Rita spent the two days having fun and enjoying their last days together. "Tina, please promise you'll come to the United States. I'll be expecting you soon," Rita said.

Tina gave Rita $9,000 for her immediate needs. They met at the airport briefly before Rita and her fake family left. They hugged and cried but were broken up by the fake mother. "It is time to go, Rita." Rita cried as she boarded the KLM plane.

Kiamu saw his name, "Uncle Kiamu," on a placard held by a beautiful young lady. He walked up to her and said, "Hi, I'm Uncle Kiamu."

Tina saw a handsome man with pink lips and the eyes of Nyenea. Instantly, she knew that he was the one. "Oh! I'm glad to see you. How was your trip?"

"I had a splendid trip, and I'm sure glad to see you."

They walked to the parked Land Rover. Kiamu saw a jeep that he'd only seen in a TV advertisement. He could not believe that he was sitting in one now. He looked around Abidjan, remembering the Africa he'd known in the seventies. *Is my country as beautiful as this place?* "Our family is very grateful for your help, and we owe you a lot. I brought you some letters from your friend."

"Thank you, sir." Tina was not sure how to relate to him because she didn't know what to say.

• • •

Dekie visited Nyenea in order to convince him to leave the country. "Hey, buddy! What's up? I'm here to talk to you about your uncle's trip. What have you decided?"

"I am not going anywhere, General. I've decided to stay with you," Nyenea replied.

"Look, little brother! I made the same mistake, and I am now deeply entrenched in our struggle today. Please reconsider your decision. You're still young."

"I've reconsidered my decision and nothing will change it—not even my uncle who I don't know. I would rather be with you than to be with some squares in the United States." Nyenea was adamant about staying in Liberia, but Dekie knew full well that the best thing for his little friend was for him to leave their death camp. He thought about himself, too. He had no one to turn to but his little friend. They shared everything, and he considered the fact that they comforted each other.

"If you have definitely decided to stay here, I'm not going to force you to change your mind, but let's live as one so others will see our unity. I also advise you to show your uncle some respect while he's here. Forget about eating human parts in your house, taking cocaine, and smoking marijuana just for these few days. You can eat human hearts at my place until he leaves."

Nyenea considered the idea for a while and said, "Thanks, man, I'm glad to be your younger brother."

They smiled, and Dekie offered his hand to Nyenea. Nyenea took his hand and held it for a long time without saying a word. He released Dekie's hand and said, "I have something to share with you as soon as my uncle leaves."

• • •

From Logatou border to Weala, the last town, Kiamu sat in the back behind the driver and looked out of the window. He saw the destruction of the towns and villages. He also saw the panic-stricken faces along the road. He could not believe that he was in Liberia. At the Salala gate, there was a man who had been accused of stealing from the market. He saw a rebel stab the man in his stomach. His intestines gushed out. The horror was enough to make Kiamu turn back, but it was too late. He only had a smooth ride because he was in a convoy of NPFL rebels. He could never leave the border and cross into Liberia alone. He would be robbed and killed in less than five minutes.

Before the turn from the main road toward Gibi, he saw a checkpoint with dozens of human skulls mounted on sticks. At the checkpoint, there were many young men and women lying on the ground face down. He saw another group beheading a young boy. He shut his eyes, but the image lingered. "Oh, God! Why did you allow me to come here?"

"Let's go now! Move the car from here quickly!" Tina urged her driver. She had noticed the despair on Kiamu's face and felt sorry for him. Kiamu's eyes were still shut when they drove into the yard. He opened his eyes when the car slowed down. "So this is why my brother-in-law could not leave his farm."

The house was very beautiful with a spectacular view of Mount Gibi and breathtaking landscape. The experience on the road momentarily left him as he beheld the beauty of the land. He felt sad about their deaths, and the thought of not meeting them in their house terrified him. Tears left his eyes as they got closer to the house. As they were ready to park, he saw acres of lands stretched out. "Wow! My brother-in-law was partly right in delaying their trip to the United States. How did he work such a big spread?" This was the best thing he had seen since their trip began.

He was still deep in his thoughts when Tina said, "Uncle Kiamu, this is the house, but I don't think your nephew is around."

He jumped out of the car. "This house is too beautiful to be out here in this jungle."

"I'm sorry about the things you saw, but it's like that around here, Uncle."

"Yeah, thanks for your concern," Kiamu said.

He was led inside and Tina showed him his room. "Uncle, if you want anything, just say it."

"No, I'll rest for a while until he returns," Kiamu said. He didn't expect anything good to be in the house, but he got the shock of his life. From the front porch to the living room and his bedroom were luxuries beyond words. In his room, he found three remote controls and didn't know what they were meant for. He punched the power button of one, and the TV came on. He hit another power button which was for the decoder, and CNN *World News* was on.

He muttered, "How can he get CNN here? I can't afford cable in the United States, and my nephew is enjoying it here." The room was a little warm so he tried to open the windows but he mistakenly hit the power button of the third remote control, and the air conditioning came on. He stood there for a long time, forgetting that he was so far from civilization.

Tina filled the refrigerator with everything that she bought from Ivory Coast. She had asked the French chap at the supermarket to give her drinks, toiletries, and anything that an American guest would love to have. Being a French citizen, the chap knew just what she needed. Nyenea had instructed them to keep the generators on day and night from his uncle's arrival until his departure. Tina knocked on the door with Kiamu's toiletries in her hands, but Kiamu was fast asleep when she entered.

Dekie and Nyenea spent the day together, talking about his uncle's visit. Nyenea was afraid to face his uncle, but his boss tried to calm him down. "Look, boy. Be yourself and tell him that you'll follow him after our coming operation in October. I'll help you get out without our leaders knowing."

Nyenea didn't know his uncle, but he'd grown up hearing his name from his mother. He knew that his mother had loved him very much and would have been very happy to see her only brother again after so many years. Tears welled up in his eyes for the first time since he heard about his uncle's visit. He and his boss, Dekie, had gotten along quite well for the past couple of months. They found solace in each other. At his age, Nyenea thought he was having fun, but after his boss made him understand the risk of being a freedom fighter, he was coming to realize that it was a game of life and death.

Dekie took him home to meet his uncle. Nyenea was so tense that he thought he would explode. Tina met him outside and hugged him, but his response was cold. He was wearing his full camouflage uniform with his rank shining on his chest and on his cap. He put on a brave face and walked straight to his uncle's room and knocked.

Kiamu was seated on the sofa, watching CNN *World News*. "Come in."

Nyenea walked in with his head bowed. "Hi, Uncle."

Kiamu got up and didn't know how to greet him. He was taken aback to see a military man standing before him. Nyenea was almost five feet seven inches tall, with a broad chest and strong muscles. "Nyenea! Come here and hug me." They embraced and held each other for a long time before Kiamu said, "I'm sorry about your parents' death. Your grandparents and sisters are all glad that you're alive." He stood back. "Look at you. You're not a child anymore. You have grown up!"

They sat down. Kiamu did all the talking. "You look just like your father. It's only your mother's eyes that you have. Oh, boy! I'm sure glad to see you. Tell me about yourself."

"I'm fine, Uncle, and how's everyone?"

"We're all fine and hoping for all of us to be together. Everyone has been crying for you," Kiamu said.

For the first time, Nyenea felt that he belonged to a family after the death of his parents.

Kiamu had decided against rushing to spell things out to Nyenea; instead he would use a softer approach on his nephew. He also found it difficult to bring up the topic after he saw the farm and the way his nephew lived. Nyenea ate good food with lots of vegetables and drank champagne everyday. He had had enough fruit juices and other drinks to make him forget his uncivilized environment. Kiamu had taken a tour around the farm, and he was happy to find the animals and chickens. The workers in the field were happy to see him mainly because he was not a rebel. He talked to James. "Did you know my sister, Polan?"

"Ah, yes! She was my madam here until they took her away."

Kiamu focused a webcam on James and told him not to tell anyone about their discussion. "Who took your madam from the farm?" Kiamu asked.

"My madam and boss were taken away by some of the freedom fighters who invaded the premises in June last year."

"What did they do to them before taking them away?"

"They were beaten and dragged from the house and put in the trunk of the fighters' car."

"Where was their son, Nyenea?"

"He was out on the farm with me."

"How did he escape?"

"I hid him in my house until General Dekie came for him two weeks later."

"Did they take anything from the house?"

"This house was completely destroyed, and they carried everything away."

"But why is the house looking new with everything intact?"

"This house was just renovated by Captain Nyenea, and everything that you see in the house was placed there just before Christmas."

"Thanks, James. Please keep our conversation to yourself."

"No fly will hear about it, sir!" James smiled and felt good to tell someone about the carnage that he witnessed. Kiamu gave him $500 and thanked him for taking Nyenea in for safety.

Kiamu wanted to see what the base looked like and how they operated. He went out the next day with Tina to tour the entire operation. The main training camp was more like a makeshift ground with sticks placed around it for a fence. He took some pictures and asked many questions. Tina loved being around him and answered his questions. He saw that many of the fighters carrying guns were between the ages of ten and fifteen. As soon as they pulled away, an old pickup truck crossed them and stopped. Kiamu was afraid when he saw five teenage boys head toward their car.

"Just sit still, Uncle. I'll handle them," Tina said and got down.

"Who's that man taking pictures of our base? Bring him out now!" a boy of about twelve commanded Tina.

"Look, he's the father of Captain Nyenea. He is visiting him. If you don't want trouble, just leave us alone right now before I call him," Tina said.

Another boy about his age came out and whispered something to the first boy "Leave me alone! She's lying! This is Lieutenant Johnson's former girlfriend. I'll teach her a good lesson today. Let the man come out at once before I shoot the car!" the boy shouted.

Kaimu tried to call Tina, but he was interrupted by gunshots. His heart pounded, and he was in a daze when he heard the gunshots.

"God, please save me from this one," he prayed. Just then, Nyenea's Nissan came from nowhere at a very high speed and hit two of the boys standing on the road, killing them instantly.

"What is this, Tina? Who's this fool standing with you?" He didn't know that his uncle was in the car.

"He wants your uncle," Tina began but before she could end the sentence, Nyenea fired ten shots into the boy scattering his brains on his old pickup. The other boys were about to run, but Nyenea ordered them back. "Take their bodies away and meet me in the office now."

Kiamu didn't know where he was when the car came to a halt.

"I'm sorry, Uncle, but if your nephew did not do that, they would have killed you," Tina said.

"That's it! I'm ready to leave this place right now," Kiamu said. He entered his room to pack his bag. He wondered how he would get out and why he had come in the first place. He got into bed, shaking like a kid. "How can my nephew live in a place like this? This is hellfire."

From that day, he decided not to go around the base until he left with his nephew. Nyenea came back that night and apologized to his uncle for his actions. "Things doesn't work as normal around here, sir. I would have gotten bad news from Tina about you today if I had not gotten there on time. Please understand."

"OK, but next time, please use another approach," Kiamu said.

"I wanted us to see Konola Mission, your former school, and Kakata," Nyenea said to defuse the situation.

Nyenea and his uncle went to Kakata with Tina and his bodyguards. Kiamu and Tina got along well as the days went by. He decided to use Tina as his bait when he noticed Nyenea's attachment to her. They went to Konola SDA Mission to see his former school campus. His former campus was filled with many young kids training for NPFL.

How can they be using the mission to train fighters when they should be opening schools for these young boys? Kiamu thought. They could not go many places as they wanted to. They left for Kakata, the capital city of Margibi County. It was overcrowded with thousands of people. There were many people standing by the road as if they were in search of someone.

"Why is the city overcrowded?" Kiamu asked.

Tina, who had lived in Kakata before she was taken to Gibi by Lt. Johnson, quickly said, "They're displaced from their towns and villages."

The trip was also a strategy for Kiamu to get to know his nephew better. He decided to spend more time with him. Since his arrival, he had not openly condemned him for his involvement in the movement. His heart sank when he saw his own people suffering so much. *I thank God that I didn't agree to support this madness in the first place. My friends who gave financial support will be shocked to see the pictures I have to show them.* There was a loud explosion in the distance that made his heart jump.

"That's Dudu bird! Let's get from here before they see us," Nyenea said. Tina turned the car around in a perfect semicircle and sped off toward Gibi.

"Strap on your seat belts!" Tina shouted as she stepped on the accelerator.

"What was that noise?" Kiamu asked.

"That's the sound of the ECOMOG planes bombing our targets around BWI campus. It's called 'Dudu bird' here," Nyenea answered. They reached the base with Kiamu's heart still pounding fast.

Kiamu got to know Dekie. He went to see him at his office and saw loneliness and dejection in Dekie's face.

"May I record our conversation on video?" Kiamu asked.

"Go ahead, Uncle. You're our guest."

"How old are you, General?"

"I'll be twenty-two years old next month."

"Ah, you're a young man! Why not a student but a soldier? And how do you run such a large military base with so many of your soldiers older than you?"

"It's easy to run. We don't have sophisticated weapons, so we use light automatic machine guns. We add a little bravery to get them going. I wanted to go to school, but the war came and destroyed my plans. I've chosen to liberate our country from corrupt politicians," Dekie answered.

"And what's that bravery that you teach your men?"

"The rules of war," Dekie responded.

"What are the rules of war?"

"Rule number one is that young men die in war, and rule number two is that you can't change rule number one. So we tell them to be vigilant." Dekie felt cool about himself after giving such a smart answer to the older man. "I have a friend in the United States with my sisters. We were drafted together, but he chose to continue his education, and I chose to free my people. You see, some had to stand up to the tyrant Samuel Doe. Anyway, here's his phone number. Please call him when you get to the United States. You may give him my pictures too." Dekie handed Kiamu some pictures along with Saye's phone number.

Kiamu was shocked to hear this kid talking about freeing his people when he needed freedom from their leaders. "Samuel Doe is no more. So who are you freeing your people from?"

"From the politicians!" Dekie answered. Their leader had to put another reason in their heads, so now he used the politicians as an excuse.

"Look, General. We're glad that you took care of our boy. The family in the United States is very grateful to you, but I must ask, don't you think that he's too young to be out here?"

"Yes, he is too young to be here. I've talked to him about leaving with you. I'm totally responsible for him here. I felt sorry after the death of his parents, who were so nice to me, but he has outgrown me now, and I can't impose my will on him. But notwithstanding, I'll talk to him again about leaving with you."

"OK, General. It was a pleasure talking with you."

"You too, Uncle."

Tina waited outside for him.

"Hey, Tina! I'm sorry I took so long."

"It's OK with me, Uncle."

"How do you feel, being young and beautiful, hanging out here in the wild?" Kiamu asked Tina.

"I want to get out. After our parents were killed in Bong Mines, we were on our own. Your nephew rescued me from a rebel who was abusing me. But I want to leave for Ghana to continue my studies. Your niece Seanee and I completed high school together. She's about to graduate while our school, Cuttington University College, is closed and instead being used by fighters today."

"How can you help me get my nephew out?"

"I can try to persuade him, but I can't force him," Tina said flatly.

"Did he send you to call Seanee the first time?"

"No, I discovered your number on the back of one of the photos, and I copied it without him knowing. He didn't know I spoke with his sister on my first trip. I later convinced him to get in touch with you all. I want him to leave this country and continue his education."

Kiamu sat in the front seat, listening to Tina. He felt good that there were a few young people with brains left in the country. "I admire your strength and courage, Tina, and if we don't see each other again, remember that I'll always respect you."

It was two days before his departure to the United States. Time was now against him. His nephew had not shown any sign of interest in leaving with him. They had some wonderful time together talking.

Kiamu finally decided it was time to break the ice. "Nyenea, your family needs you. Please come with me to the United States, and we'll come back after the war to rebuild this farm." Kiamu felt as if he was standing before a judge waiting for a verdict. Time felt like it stopped while he awaited his nephew's answer. *I've risked my life against all odds. Will it be for nothing? What will I tell his grandparents and sisters if he refuses to leave?*

"Uncle, I want to come with you, but I'll follow later."

Kiamu felt sweat pouring down his back. He didn't know what to say or think anymore. He didn't come all the way here to hear this. Anger washed over him. He wanted to shout but held himself back. "Nyenea, your mother was my best friend and sister. I loved her so much that I would do anything for her. I asked them to leave this farm when the war started, and your father refused to leave. Today, the farm is still here, and they are both dead. Please don't make the same mistake they made. I'm here in person, not faraway talking to you on phone. Let's leave this place for a better and brighter future."

His words cut deep into Nyenea's heart. He tried to recall his parents' attitude when the war came closer and how his father's failure to take him and his mother away led to their demise. His anger rose against his dead father like a storm. "He killed my mother! My father killed my mother!" Nyenea cried for a long time and then sat quietly.

His uncle moved over and held his hands. "I'm sorry about your mom, but don't blame your father for that. It's in the past now. Your family is waiting for you in the United States. You can complete your studies and have a better future."

Nyenea walked out of his uncle's room without looking back, climbed into his pickup truck, and drove away as fast as possible, leaving dust behind him.

Tina came in to see Kiamu. "How was your discussion?"

"He's not willing to leave this place. He has too much money and authority to let go," Kiamu said.

"I'm sorry, Uncle."

Nyenea left and was not seen for two days. His uncle waited for another two days without seeing him. He sent his bodyguards with a letter to Tina instructing her to give his uncle $200,000 for his sisters. He was on a mission in Tubmanburg, Bomi County, and would not be back soon. Tina explained to Kiamu, but he just could not understand why his nephew was behaving like this. "I can't accept any money from him, Tina, and I'll leave without him!"

Tina checked where he said he had the money and was shocked to see such a large amount of cash. Her eyes were wide as she stared at the green bills of US dollars. *This is my chance for freedom. I'll take it all, or a lot, and leave with a one-way ticket.* She sat down and counted the money, imagining herself as a teller in a bank. Five hundred thousand dollars in hundred-dollar bills! She took out the $200,000 and put it in her suitcase. She packed some of her best clothes and two pairs of shoes. Nyenea had instructed her to take $10,000 for her trip and for the purchase of provisions.

Before leaving, Kiamu decided to contact Dekie, but he too had gone to Bomi. They had left that morning with their escort and bodyguards. Kiamu was deep in his thoughts as the car went on. *What will I tell his grandparents?*

He had taken one last look at the house and farmland and wondered whether this was his last view of his sister's property. Before getting to

Salala gate, they learned that the rebel leader was coming with a huge convoy. As they parked their cars, Kiamu stared out of the window, wanting to see the rebel leader.

"The president is coming!" announced their driver. The rebel leader got down at the gate, completely surrounded by his bodyguards. Kiamu could not see him, but he managed to take few photos of the scene.

At the border in Logatou, Tina asked the escort to return to the base. The escort was puzzled, but the men obeyed as they were trained to do. By the time they reached Danane, it was already eight o'clock. They went to her usual motel to spend the night. Tina gave her two bodyguards $1,000 each. "I'll be doing few things in Abidjan, so I'm paying your motel bills for a week. If you don't see me, you can leave without me." Her bodyguards, Kolinkay and Johnny, had been planning to run away. Kolinkay asked her if she was coming back. He told her that they had planned not to return to Liberia and asked if she could please help them with some money for school.

"Where do you want to go?"

"Ghana," they said together.

"Get in the car with me. We will all go to Ghana together," Tina said before turning to the driver, "How about you?"

"I'm not going back. I'll stay here with my family in Boauke," the driver said.

"OK, since you have a driver's license, you'll take us to Ghana and return to your family."

Tina knocked on Kiamu's door.

"You may enter," Kiamu said.

"I'm sorry to tell you, but I'm not going back to Liberia."

Kiamu was shocked. "Are you sure of what you're saying?"

"Yes, I tried to convince your nephew to leave with me but to no avail. He's looking at those looted goods as property and wealth. I'll get back in school and be someone better in the future."

"That's a good decision, Tina. Go back to school and complete your studies. But where do you intend to live?"

"Ghana—and you know what? My bodyguards refuse to return as well, so we're going together. My driver is coming back here to live with his family in Boauke after taking us to Ghana. I'm sorry, but I can't keep risking my life for your nephew anymore."

It was so much news in a relatively short time that it was difficult for Kiamu to digest. "Well, I wish my nephew would think like these young ones and come with me and go back to school."

The trip to Abidjan was cheerful. Everyone was laughing and throwing jokes here and there. There was no more "Oma," as she was referred to in Gibi. Tina warned them against using such a name and that no one should mention her past.

Kiamu left that night for the United States. Tina and her crew slept in the Concorde Hotel. It was the boys' first time in such a beautiful hotel. They were stared at as if they were aliens. The next morning, they left for the Ghanaian border and crossed into Elubu, Ghana. Tina dropped the boys at the Buduburam refugee camp and gave them $2,000 each. "I'll come to visit you guys. Take care and stay out of trouble. As soon as you get in school, let me know. Bye."

● ● ●

The new rebel faction from Sierra Leone had been cutting NPFL control from Bomi and Cape Mount Counties. Dekie's forces were badly beaten back from Tubmanburg, with many of them killed and wounded. He retreated and took his forces back to base. After a week of fighting, he had lost more than two hundred of his best fighters. Nyenea was slightly injured in the arm. He was taken to Rennie Hospital in Kakata. When he returned, he learned that Tina had not returned from Ivory Coast yet. When he saw her escort car he thought she was back, but the escort said they were instructed by Tina to return to base once they arrived at the border.

Nyenea was beside himself. He could not see himself living without Tina. Her presence had changed him for the better. He started using hard drugs excessively every day. Tina had made him think like a normal human being but in her absence, he didn't care anymore. "I'll wait for another week before I send someone to check on her."

He met Dekie to discuss her absence. "Just calm down and wait. Tina will be back as soon as she gets some things done. You know ladies and how concerned they are about their beauty. Maybe, she's getting some suits made before coming home."

• • •

Saye was in his final year at the University of Michigan. He was now a professional journalist with a local daily. When he was a kid, his dream was to work for the state-run radio, ELBC, in Liberia. But now he aimed to be a world-class journalist with VOA, CNN, *TIME* magazine, or BBC. His thesis was about African child soldiers and how they are used in conflicts on the African continent. He had difficulty writing about child soldiers from Liberia. He wanted to write about his friend Dekie and how he rose from nowhere to the rank of a general in one year, but he didn't have pictures or the proof to support his claims. Saye had contacted some news sources in Monrovia but even they didn't have sufficient evidence. He was determined to write about the brutality that had besieged his beloved country. He had already written extensively on child soldiers in the Ugandan, Sudanese, and Angolan conflicts, but he had nothing much about his own country, Liberia.

Kiamu's return to the United States was the worst time of his life. He feared meeting his parents, who were expecting him to bring Nyenea. He didn't call them from Ivory Coast to avoid questions that he could not answer. He was not met at the airport by anyone because no one knew of his return to the United States.

He arrived at the house with his luggage and rang the doorbell. His mother answered the door. She had been waiting for her son and grandson since Kiamu left for Liberia.

"Hey, Kiamu!" she quickly hugged him and moved around him to meet her grandson.

"Mom, please come back inside. I came alone." He felt drained and empty as those words came out of him. He had dreaded this meeting all the way from Africa, and now he could not avoid the sad look in his mother's eyes.

His mother burst into tears. The thought of not seeing her grandson again hit her so hard that her weeping was uncontrollable.

"I'm sorry, Mama, but we should talk first before you continue crying like that." He understood quite well the importance his mother attached to her grandson after the death of her only daughter. Nyenea was seen as the comfort for everyone since the news of his being alive surfaced. She cried as if Nyenea were dead.

Old man Sumo was ill, but he made his way downstairs when he heard his wife screaming. "What is it, my dear? Oh, you guys are here. Where's our boy?"

Kiamu could not answer his father's question. "Dad, we have to talk." It was all he could say to his father. Kiamu could not face his nieces, who had come home from school.

Kiamu explained to everyone about his trip. "Seanee, your friend Tina was a big help to me. I spent almost two weeks on the farm with Nyenea and Tina. We went out to Kakata." He knew what everyone wanted to hear, and he took time to spill it out. "I talked to Nyenea about coming with me, but he refused and walked out. We didn't meet again until I left. He said not now, but he would come later this year."

"Why couldn't you grab him and bring him by force?" his mom asked.

"Mom, Nyenea is not a kid anymore. He's the rebel deputy commander responsible for thousands of men and women. He has bodyguards all over his house and they are all well armed. We can only hope that he comes to his senses. His girlfriend, Tina, talked to him, but he refused to listen to her. Tina came with me to Ivory Coast and ran away to Ghana with her bodyguards and driver. She's gone to Ghana to continue her studies. Our Nyenea is not thinking like them, I'm afraid."

The house was silent as everyone listened to him. There were tears in his nieces' eyes. They all cried and wailed as if nothing could comfort them anymore. "I'm sorry for not bringing him, but you can see the pictures later and a video I have of him and his boss, General Dekie. Please try to study hard and get yourself prepared to rescue our country. Liberia is damaged, destroyed by children turned into soldiers. If I had not gotten an escort to take me into Liberia, I would have stayed at the border. Your friend Tina was instrumental in making sure my stay was wonderful," Kiamu said. "The house is more beautiful than ours. The front porch and the interior are beautifully designed with expensive decorations. I watched CNN out there on the farm."

• • •

Nyenea went back into his shell when he finally realized that Tina wasn't coming back. He and Dekie always celebrated July 26, but that was not even mentioned. He didn't care about himself anymore. Dekie noticed his absentmindedness but could not do much to help. He tried to get closer to him so they could comfort each other. They took drugs together and had sex with multiple teenage girls. As a sadist, Nyenea harmed people, and he went on striking anyone who came his way.

Dekie's marines were ready for the operation that had taken so long to plan and prepare for. One evening as they sat taking cocaine, Nyenea said, "General Dudu wants me to assassinate you." Dekie was already dazed and high after injecting himself, so he didn't quite understand what Nyenea said.

Nyenea repeated his words to his boss.

Then it hit Dekie. "What! When did all that start?"

"On our first trip to the Gbarnga. He promised to give me $100,000 and your position as the commander here after I did the job."

As Nyenea spoke, Dekie's mind went far back to his first challenge with the general in Butowou and the words of his friend, Mosquito, rang in his mind. "Be careful with him after today!" Dekie told the story to Nyenea. "I thought it was done with, but he still has a grudge against me. So what do you want to do?"

"Let me know what you want me to do, boss, because I'm ready to waste him."

Dekie felt good about his boy's statement. "OK, boy! Since he wants to get me, we'll get him. We'll meet in Kakata before the operation. Take him aside and pretend to still be in for the deal. When you two are alone, take him out!"

Dekie and his forces got busy planning the final touches for the great operation.

Nyenea felt good being with his only friend and boss. He occasionally thought about his uncle's visit. He didn't want to go to the United States because he could no longer fit into normal society. He knew that his sisters and grandparents were right, but he had chosen the path of destruction and death. Like his boss and mentor, he found joy in what he did, but nobody understood. He knew that he was never going to see his family again. *If I die in this coming operation or if anything happens to me, that'll be the end of me. At least, I gave them some money.*

He picked up his family album and slowly went through all the photos. He remembered when he was a kid and how his sisters always protected him. *Maybe if my sisters had come, I would have left, but for now I'm a soldier.* The money he thought he sent to them became a mystery to him and his uncle, but no one except Tina could explain it. So the $200,000 rejected by Kiamu became Tina's without a trace.

Tina was admitted to the University of Ghana's Legon Campus. She bought a house in East Legon. She was happy to be in school again after wasting two years. She thought of Nyenea and how much she missed him, but they lived in two different worlds now. She had enough money to fund her education. She invested in saloons in Accra with a Ghanaian partner.

She visited her former bodyguards, whom she found in class at the Buduburam high school in the refugee camp. They were glad to see her after a few months in Ghana. "I've started school in Legon. I'll take you some other time to see my place."

She paid for all their requirements and promised to pay their university fees also. As she drove from the camp, it dawned on her that it wasn't everyone who wanted to be a part of the country's destruction. "Those boys look so much cuter in their school uniforms than in rebel rags."

She called her friend Seanee, and they had a nice time talking on the phone. "I'm really sorry about your brother, pal. He's one hard nut to crack."

"Yeah, thanks for all the assistance. My uncle is really proud of you." Seanee said.

Tina gave her phone number to Seanee. Her sister Rita wasn't happy about her being in Ghana, but Tina promised to visit her during her break. "And I'll come to the United States to do my master's degree."

When Kiamu printed the pictures he took in Liberia, he saw five good shots of the rebel leader. He was amazed that he got a shot of him. He took time to adjust after his trip to his homeland. He couldn't believe that he had actually traveled to Liberia and returned in one piece. He thought of Tina and how she had helped him during his stay there. Her determination to move on with life and leave the temporary enjoyment that she had at her disposal surprised him. As he thought about his time also with the most feared Gen. Dekie, he thought of his letter and pictures for his friend in the United States. He went through everything and got out the pictures and the phone number.

He dialed the number, but nobody picked up. He dialed again an hour later, but no one answered. At 5:00 p.m. he dialed again and reached Saye.

"I'm Kiamu. I returned from Liberia a few weeks ago. I have a letter and some photos for you from your friend Dekie. I met him at his base in Gibi."

Saye moved around the house as if he had seen a ghost after his conversation with Kiamu.

They met Kiamu a week later. "Why do you have so much interest in the name Dekie?" Kiamu asked.

"He's a good friend of mine. You see, we grew up together. He and I were in the same class until his father's death in 1988. I completed high school before him in 1989 because there was no one to pay his school fees.

His sisters are here with me," said Saye. He told Kiamu about the forced recruitment and how he got to the United States.

Kiamu listened and asked a few questions. Kiamu also told his story from the beginning of the civil war to how his sister and brother-in-law died. "I went in to get my nephew who is now your friend's deputy. He's only seventeen years old, and he's a captain. I have a video of your friend and many pictures of children carrying guns for the NPFL."

"I'm writing my thesis on the topic of child soldiers and how they're used throughout Africa. If you don't mind, I could use your pictures and your nephew as my case study from Liberia."

"I have no problem with that. I want the world to know about the atrocities committed by those hoodlums who call themselves rebel leaders, and I'll support you in any way possible," Kiamu said.

On October 23 1992, the city of Monrovia woke up to the sound of rockets from every entry point of the city and heavy machine gunfire. The rockets landed on homes, in streets, on schools, markets, hospitals, and offices. The ground troops of Gen. Dekie came in from Pipeline to the seventy-Second barracks on Somalia Drive. They overran the ECOMOG positions and planted Capt. Nyenea and some of his death squads in the marshland close to Providence Island. The residents of Monrovia fled in every direction as rockets exploded.

The rebel leader got word that the operation was going as planned. By the end of the day, his forces would take the city and bring his entourage into power. But there was another disturbing report: the corpse of Lt. Gen. Wonbin Dudu had been found in Kakata late last night. The rebel leader had a lot on his mind, and he couldn't let such bad news break his spirit, but he had known this man for a long time in their struggle. They had trained together in Libya, and it was his late friend and others who had rescued him from prison in Ghana. There were tears in his eyes, but he held them back until he was alone. Then he cried like a baby in his office. *Who could have done this? How did such a fine brave soldier die without a fight? The assassin must be a professional.*

The rebel leader was expected to make a statement to his people about the ongoing campaign on his radio station. "My people, we have captured Monrovia from the evil forces of ECOMOG or ECUMOG or CUCUMOG. The residents of Monrovia can now gather at these centers for food rations: the Sports Commission on Broad Street, Newport High School, and Tubman High School. I thank you."

His greatest weapon against the people under his control was his mouth and the propaganda lies that he constantly fed to the citizens.

At the end of the day, the rebels were pushed back from the city. There were still pockets of Dekie's marine rebels led by Nyenea in the swamps; they were trapped. If they came out without their weapons as civilians, they would be detected because of the muddy soil that covered their bodies. Nyenea thought of every military trick in the book, but he had no solution to their predicament. He called Dekie to send a rescue team to get them out.

Dekie tried to send Lt. Johnson to lead the rescue team, but he turned the assignment down and walked away in the presence of the general's subordinates.

"If you take one more step, I'll blow your head off!" Dekie had threatened. Lt. Johnson and Nyenea had their personal problems, but that didn't warrant him disrespecting their commander with the operation failing rapidly by the hour. Gen. Dekie blew off Johnson's head, and his brains scattered on the leaves. He shook as if it was his first time doing such a thing. "Throw him away." He asked two of his best men to follow him. They went through Pipeline to SKD Boulevard and burst into the swamp by three o'clock that morning. He met Capt. Nyenea with only five men.

"What happened to the rest of your troop?" Gen. Dekie asked.

"They died from ECOMOG shelling. We had twenty wounded, but I killed them in order to move faster. That's why we were able to get this far, sir!" Capt. Nyenea said.

"OK, we have to get back to Bentol and join the rest before five thirty."

It was difficult for most of the men to keep going as they were exhausted from the heat. Many of them had leeches sucking on them.

Their heavy shoes in the mud held them back. No one could walk faster. It was a step at a time. With every step, they needed strength to pull their legs up and take the next step. Already, some had started saying that they could not carry on. Nyenea decided then to kill the five boys who complained. Dekie tried to stop him, but it was too late. The five boys shook as the bullets blew their heads off.

As soon as the ECOMOG peacekeepers saw the gunfire flames, they resumed firing at their position. The shelling was heavy, and they all ran for cover. The two boys accompanying Dekie were torn to pieces by a direct hit.

"Nyenea, let's move!" Dekie held him up as they ran. They left their guns behind. Dekie tried to call Gen. Mosquito for help, but he was running and breathing too heavily to be understood, and the radio fell from him.

"Dekie, are you OK?" Mosquito asked. He heard a big blast, and the radio went off with a big bang. Instantly, Mosquito knew the fate of the young friend he had turned into a dangerous monster. He looked at the radio for a long time and cursed their leader for starting this operation that was destroying so many of their men.

The rockets hit them as they tried to locate their radio. It blew them away without a trace. Early, the next morning, ECOMOG sent in troops to mop up the swamp in case there were still pockets of rebel resistance trapped there. But only blood and body parts were found with old shoes and slippers. The city of Monrovia was cleared of all threats from the madness of NPFL thugs once again.

It was reported on the rebel radio that the marine base lost its leader and deputy in the operation. The base was the worst hit of all in the operation. But the movement went on to serve its purpose without them as the rebels claimed to liberate Liberians from the politicians in the city of Monrovia. The decisions of these two young boys who were loved by their families brought on their own demise. It grieved all parents to see their own end up like that, but it was a force of evil that their leaders used in conjuring their children into this madness.

Saye informed the girls of Dekie's death. "It was reported on the rebel radio station a week ago that he died in the operation that killed so many civilians in Monrovia. I'm deeply sorry to be the one to break such terrible news to you all. But let's move on with life and help support Ma Yah in these dark hours."

They called Ma Yah and tried to comfort her. Ma Yah tried hard to accept her son's decision, but she just could not understand why he chose to live like that. She mourned for a month. All over Danane, people talked about their deaths. Some heaved sighs of relief because they were victims of their terror.

Kiamu was told about his nephew's death by Tina. "They died in Operation Octopus, Uncle. Please, extend my heartfelt condolences to your nieces. I'm very sorry that it turned out that way."

"Yeah, I was expecting this news, but not so soon. Anyway, we all tried to help, but he failed to see what we saw. Thanks again, Tina. We'll always be grateful for your help. Please continue your education. Bye. Keep in touch." Kiamu hung up and sat until his mother came down.

"Is he dead? I dreamed last night that he died in a river as he tried to escape from people pursuing him. I've been mourning his death since you returned. That pain will remain in my heart till I die. I'm sorry for blaming you after your trip, son," Ma Leneh said. She tried to be strong but found it impossible when she was alone. She grieved his death and cried daily for hours. Her husband began to worry.

The girls mourned their brother's death as if he had died in their arms. It was too hard for them to accept his decision to stay in the jungle and fight for something he had no knowledge of. They cried often and together when they were in their room. Kiamu and his father were the comforters in the house.

"He destroyed himself, Uncle," Neneh said as she beat the sofa next to her.

Kiamu thought long. *I wish I had kidnapped him and brought him with me, but I tried by risking my life out there. When everyone was getting out to safety, I was going into danger. My sister, if you're hearing me, please don't blame me too.*

Saye and his household had the worst Christmas since their arrival. Ma Yah's health deteriorated as the death of her son hit her so hard. There were constant calls to Ivory Coast. Saye had asked Quianue and his mom to do everything possible to calm her. It was 1993, his final semester, and he focused on his thesis. He wrote extensively about the Liberian child soldiers and their abuse by the rebel leaders and the self-destruction brought on themselves in the process. He used Nyenea as a case study. Kiamu gave him lots of help, as he had promised. He presented a case on the Liberian conflict that many Westerners never thought was possible. The cannibalistic nature of the rebel group shocked the world. He tried to show why these young boys and girls ate other human beings. Their quest for human flesh was due to propaganda spread by their leaders that it was a talisman that made them strong and safe from other human spirits. The ghosts of people they killed would never hurt them as long as they were eating human hearts and lungs. His thesis was completed and presented to his supervisor.

A month later, he called Kiamu to tell him the good news. "Thanks, Uncle, for your assistance. I submitted my thesis, and the school is talking about a possible publication of it in major journals around the world. I'm inviting you to my convocation." Kiamu was happy to hear about such a success story from a determined young man. "I'll be there, come what may," Kiamu promised.

At the convocation, Saye was honored as a success story from Africa. After the program, he and Lulu announced their engagement date and invited everyone to the party.

"Congratulations!"

Saye turned and saw Kiamu. "Thank you, sir, and thanks for coming." They shook hands and talked for a while.

He got a letter from the Associated Press (AP), inviting him for an interview. He was given a job to investigate the abuse of child soldiers in

Africa. He was assigned to their Johannesburg bureau in South Africa. Saye and Lulu had their engagement party and traveled to Danane for the wedding because of Ma Yah's failing health and as a way of spending time with their parents. The wedding brought a lot of joy to both Ma Yah and Ma Kou. Their wedding was the biggest wedding ever held in Danane. Saye asked Ma Yah to consider him as her own son.

Two weeks after the wedding, he left for South Africa. The two mothers rejoiced; their children's marriage renewed their hope for a brighter future. The pain that Ma Yah felt was healed, and her health was restored with the presence of her daughters. The girls and Yeanue returned to the United States to complete their studies, leaving behind their happy mothers.

END

29281625R00083

Made in the USA
Middletown, DE
13 February 2016